#LoveOzYA Short Stories

Underdog

WITH A FOREWORD BY FLEUR FERRIS

Edited by Tobias Madden
and Sarah Taviani

Underdog

First published in Australia in 2019
by Underdog Books
underdogshortstories.com
underdogshortstories@outlook.com

ISBN: 9781760641344 (paperback)
eISBN: 9781743820797 (ebook)

A catalogue record for this book is available from the National Library of Australia

Contents

Foreword

by Fleur Ferris

Many years ago, when I decided I wanted to be a police officer, one quick phone call to the recruiting office told me there was a set procedure to follow to make it happen. The method was tried and tested, and every police officer before and after me also followed it—it wouldn't be easy, but if I worked hard and passed the application and training processes, I would make it through. It was the same when I decided to be a paramedic: there was an application process to follow, study to do, exams to pass, rules to obey, and specified requirements to meet before I could succeed. This was the case for every set goal in my life, until I decided I wanted to be a traditionally-published author.

After reading numerous author blogs and interviews, I realised I had thrown myself into a world of uncertainty. It seemed no author's 'getting published' story was the same as another's. There isn't even regularity in the submission process. Each agency and publisher has their own dos and don'ts, and even if you research and follow the set submission guidelines, there are still no guarantees of success.

I'm the type of person who loves concrete evidence—research, formulas, science, facts—yet, this industry I wanted to get into offered none of these things. This is what I knew:

1) There are published authors in the world.

2) Authors are people.

3) I'm a person.

4) Therefore, I have a chance.

Optimism is everything! But, now what?

I attended festivals, did workshops and courses, listened to agents, publishers and published authors on panels, read a lot and, of course, wrote a lot. I found other writers with similar goals and exchanged critiques with them. I did whatever I could to improve my craft, and while I felt like I was bombarded with choices about how to get published, my research told me success boiled down to three things: the right manuscript had to land on the right desk at the right time.

Right manuscript + Right desk + Right time = Publishing contract

I looked at each component of this equation.

Right manuscript – What is the *right manuscript*? There is no set science for this. Publishers may not even know what they are looking for until they read it. I couldn't predict publishing trends, and even if I could, I wouldn't want to write to order. I figured all I could do was write the very best version of the story that set my heart on fire, the story only I could write, and hope for the best.

Right desk – With no contacts in the publishing world, I had no clue how to find the *right desk*, but I knew a good agent could help with this. A good agent will have good relationships with publishers and should know what types of stories which publishers are looking for. Finding an agent didn't give 100% certainty of getting published, but it increased my odds of finding that right desk.

Right time – I had no way of knowing when it was the *right time* to submit my work. My focus returned to agents. An agent knows what type of books are selling and therefore will also know when it's the best time to submit a story.

My decision was made—I would concentrate my efforts on finding an agent.

Just before I was about to start submitting my work, I attended another writers festival. One piece of advice from a publishing panel stuck with me:

If you want to find an agent before submitting your work to a publisher, do your research and find the agent most likely to like your work, then aim and shoot your submission like an arrow to that agent.

For me, the rest is history. I found an agent who loves and champions my work, my novel was picked up by a brilliant publisher, and a wonderful working relationship with them began.

To the driven and dedicated writers out there who aspire to be published, please know that with the uncertainty comes unlimited possibilities, and this is the most exciting and inspiring thing. I hope you all find the perfect launch pad for your writing career, and that boundless and thrilling opportunities follow.

Bravo to each and every one of the writers published in this anthology; there is nothing sweeter than seeing your work in print for the first time, and *Underdog* is now a part of your 'getting published' story.

Wishing you all almighty and ongoing success, whatever that means for you.

Meet and Greet

BY

MICHAEL EARP

My inner fanboy is clawing his way up my throat. If he gets out, there'll be a hurricane of squeals and nervous jazz hands ripping this room to shreds.

Keep it in check, Cooper. Keep that locked down.

My geek is hard to harness. And now that I'm actually in the same room as Matthias Brown it's bucking like a full-grown unicorn. I'm sure he did a longitudinal survey of my entire life and decided to write a novel. Even the main character is called Cooper. It's uncanny, and slightly unsettling, but entirely life-affirming.

I can't believe how jumpy I am and the talk hasn't even started. To pass the time, I take a photo—about a million photos—of Matthias sitting on stage. I've snagged a seat in the second row so I have a pretty good view. He's chatting quietly with the person who'll be interviewing him. The irregular glass shapes that make up the wall behind him let in heaps of light and glimpses of the trees lining the river. For all their strange angles, the Federation Square buildings feel like they belong. But I guess they've always been a part of my Melbourne.

I scroll through my pics, stopping when I find the best one. He must have been scanning the crowd, and I captured him as he was looking right in my direction. He's smiling as if he's posing for me. I crop it, edit the filters a little, and post it online.

> **coopdegrace** OMG! I am less than 10m away from @matthiaswrites right now! FREAKING OUT!!!!

I'm so excited I forget to say where I am or use any hashtags.

Oh well, it can go out to my 247 followers; I'm sure they'd know by now how much this means to me. My feed is overrun with pictures of *Things I Forgot to Say* or quotes from it. All Matthias's book, all the time. I sank in deep, that's for sure.

My phone buzzes. Someone's commented already.

> **aboymadeofbooks** I'm jel! You got a much better seat than I did! I'm stuck right up the back.

I smile, proud of myself. As if I wasn't going to get here an hour early to be as close to the front as possible. Also, a little bit proud ABoyMadeOfBooks commented on my post. He's got nearly ten thousand followers and takes stunning photos. I didn't realise he'd be here. I wonder if he lives in Melbourne too. I'd been commenting on his posts for ages before he followed me back. He's got great taste in books but, clearly, I love *Things I Forgot to Say* more.

I turn around to try and see him, not that I know what he looks like. He's not in his pics, they're all about the books. The theatre is packed now, there are even people standing at the back.

The lights dim and the music goes off.

Forget ABoyMadeOfBooks, I'm here for Matthias!

The talk begins and I BLISS OUT. I'm laughing too loudly at his jokes, and when he talks about where the story came from I blush when he doesn't say it was based on my life. But I don't care—no one's paying any attention to me.

During question time, I want to ask if he knows how real his characters are, but I'm petrified of the idea of the microphone in my face. So, I listen to the other questions and roll my eyes when someone asks why he made Scott move away from Cooper at the end. I want to stand up and scream, 'Were you not listening to him? What else could have happened after all that?' But I don't. You know, stage fright and all.

Someone asks about Toby, a minor character who comes in at the end. I've always been too fixated on the raw, Scott-shaped hole in Cooper's life to pay much attention to anyone who entered the story after Scott left.

I feel like I'm floating when it ends, but I quickly hit the ground when I remember the signing line. I make it to the end of my row and then push my way past everyone as if it were a medical emergency. There's a bottleneck at the door and I try not to hyperventilate.

Once I'm in the queue, maybe twenty people from the front, I breathe normally again. I take out my copy of *Things I Forgot to Say* and flip through it. Suddenly I'm afraid to show it to Matthias. The cover is already curling and the corners are bent. The girl in front of me is sliding her brand-new copy out of a paper bag and I can't help but think mine looks spoiled and tatty. Should I have bought a new copy? I flip through it and see one of the lines I've underlined in the second half.

This is who I am. Didn't you see me?

I take a deep breath. I'm okay with my copy being a bit worn—fine, a lot worn. It's only because I love it so much.

I feel my phone buzz again. ABoyMadeOfBooks is DMing me.

Are you wearing a green denim jacket?

I glance down at my clothes to answer what I already know. Yes, I am. I don't know if I'm creeped out or flattered.

Yeah, why?

I hit send and wait for a reply. Instead I get a tap on my shoulder.

Turning, I see the next boy in line smiling at me. He's got short dark hair and olive skin. He's about my age and breathtaking.

'You're CoopDeGrace, right? I'm ABoyMadeOfBooks.'

If boys are made of books, all the books in my stomach are flying off their shelves.

'But I thought you were older?' Did that really come out of my mouth? How is that the first thing I say to him?

He laughs. It's a beautiful sight, even though I'm mortified he's laughing at something stupid I said.

'What made you think that?' he asks.

'Your account, I guess. You've got so many followers, I assumed you were older.'

'I'm only fifteen.'

'Oh, me too.'

'There you go.'

'But I don't have ten thousand followers, and get so many likes and comments.'

He laughs again. 'It's only a bit over eight thousand, and that's not important. I just love reading books and love taking photos of them.'

'You're pretty amazing at it.'

'Thanks.' He shifts from foot to foot, like he doesn't like being the centre of attention. 'So, you must be pretty excited.' He nods to the front of the queue where Matthias is taking a seat and saying hello to the first person.

I remember why I'm here again for the first time in two minutes and my inner unicorn bucks happily, right into my guts. How is it that I forgot, even for a second?

'I can't even!' I say, my voice small and tight with excitement.

'Yeah,' he says, '*Things* was okay.'

My face drops and I cloud over suddenly like Melbourne weather. 'What?'

He's laughing again. 'The look on your face! Obviously, I loved it too. I'm here, aren't I?'

I'm about to snap at him for scaring me like that when a woman walks up to us holding a pad of post-its and a black marker. 'Are you getting books dedicated today? What name would you like them made out to?'

ABoyMadeOfBooks indicates for me to go first.

'Cooper,' I say, suddenly registering the fact that Matthias Brown is about to write *my* name in my copy of *his* book.

The woman says, 'Like in the book?'

I nod.

ABoyMadeOfBooks nods too. 'Amazing. And here I was thinking you misspelled your handle.'

I exhale sharply, day-time-TV-scandalised. Like I'd make that mistake.

The woman hands me the post-it and I put it inside the front cover of my book. She turns to ABoyMadeOfBooks.

'Brodie,' he says.

She writes it down and says, 'For a second I thought you were going to say Scott and that would have been too cute!'

Is there a fire in the room? The heat in my face says so. Brodie is cute, but more than one 'Scott' in my life is not cute at all. I'm glad when she moves on to the next person in the queue.

Brodie—his real name is like a secret, just for me—seems quiet for a second. Is he blushing too? It's hard to tell. A grin sneaks back onto his face and he says, 'So you've been obsessing over this book for a while. What are you going to say to him?'

I turn to look at Matthias, signing books, smiling for photos with people. 'I'm not sure I'll be able to say much at all,' I say honestly. I don't add, 'Which is why I've got a letter I wrote tucked inside the back cover of my book ready to give to him.'

'Come on! If you don't think of something now, you'll either clam up, or gush embarrassingly and overshare.'

I hold my book close to my chest, thinking of the letter. Is it oversharing? Is it too much to say I'd gone through the same thing as Book-Cooper? And that knowing someone else had, and had come through it okay, made me feel at peace with myself? Even if that person was a fictional character? I feel the same way as Book-Cooper about so many things and I'm not fictional. So, the rest doesn't matter at all. It's vital.

'I guess I'll say I loved his book.'

This boy is making me second-guess my plan of attack. Not that I had one. It was more like Matthias was a target and I hurtled myself towards him without thinking out the details, and now, when I'm finally within feet of reaching that target, someone has turned my head.

The queue is moving quicker than I thought it would. We're only five people from the front now and my nerves are kicking in, full strength.

Pats unicorn *Settle boy, settle.*

It's almost enough to forget ABoyMadeOfBooks is talking to me like we're old friends, like I'm worth noticing when I'm so small in his big world. Almost.

With nerves crashing over me from both sides, I'm now at the front of the queue, next in line.

The girl in front slides her book out of the paper bag and says to Matthias, 'I'm looking forward to reading it.'

I'm equal parts dismissive and jealous. Why she hasn't read it yet is beyond me, but what I wouldn't give to read it for the first time again. That instant recognition. That spark of myself lighting up the pages.

It's my turn. My stomach drops like the floor opened. I can picture my unicorn falling through space, nothing left to buck against. I step forward and slide my book across the table towards Matthias.

'Hey there—' he opens the cover to see the post-it with my name on it '—Cooper! No way!'

All I can manage to say is, 'Yeah.'

Rather than signing straight away, he inspects the book. 'Woah, this is well read!' He's flipping through the pages, seeing my dog-ears and my underlining. Occasionally I'd even written in the margins. I'm kicking myself! Why didn't I buy a fresh copy for him to sign? 'How many times have you read this, Cooper?'

'Um, eight, I think.' I'm so aware of Brodie listening in, hearing me speak in broken clauses. The fact he's on my mind when I'm *finally* talking to Matthias Brown is annoying and confusing.

'It's only been out for six months.'

'I only discovered it two months ago.' I'm so proud to get a complete sentence out. Ms Grady, the librarian at school, had put it in my hand. I read it that night, staying up till three in the morning. I forced Dad to take me to a bookshop the next day. I *needed* my own copy.

Matthias is flipping through that exact copy now, looking at the bits I've marked. Like I handed him my diary, even though he wrote it. He gets to the back and the envelope falls out.

'Oh, that's for you.' I forgot all about the letter in my frenzy of emotions.

He looks right at me. 'Thank you.'

I feel like we've connected, like he gets it, gets how I'm feeling, and I didn't even gush or anything. He slides the envelope into the bag under his seat and opens the book to the title page. I watch him writing in the book that means so much to me. It has been a lifeline, a buoy in the sea of crap I've been feeling since all that mess went down. A crutch, maybe, but a comfort, too. I don't allow myself to concentrate on what he's writing because I'm afraid I'll cry if I read it. He closes the cover and holds the book a little longer.

'Thank you for coming out to meet me today, Cooper.'

I'm about to speak when Brodie is at my shoulder. 'Give us your phone,' he says to me, before asking Matthias, 'Can Cooper get a picture with you?'

'Of course!'

I'm in a daze and Brodie ushers me around the signing table. I find myself next to Matthias and he stands up and puts his arm across my shoulders. I must be smiling like a kid in a bookshop because my face is aching. Hopefully I don't look too manic. Hopefully Brodie will take more than one. But he's a pro, I'm sure he's used to taking more than one.

When Brodie lowers his arms, Matthias shakes my hand. 'It was nice to meet you.'

I nod my head. 'You too. I love your book.'

He laughs once. 'I can tell. It makes me happy to hear it.'

He hands me my book and I step aside to let Brodie get his signed.

I realise, as I'm standing there, that there's no tangible reason for me to wait for Brodie. We didn't come here together, we don't really know each other, other than a few online exchanges.

But I want to.

I want to share with him how it felt to meet the author of my favourite book. I want to hear more from him about the books he loves—beyond the few words that go with his beautiful photos. I want his smile to be directed at me, to hear him laugh again.

So, I wait.

He comes towards me and I say, 'Crap! I didn't offer to take a photo for you.'

He waves his hand. 'Don't worry about it, I hate being in front of the camera.'

I'm about to protest further when he bumps me with his shoulder. 'I'm starving! Let's get something to eat.' I stare at him, not moving. 'Sorry,' he says, 'You probably have somewhere you need to be.'

'No.'

'Then what?'

I've got the biggest urge to say, 'But why do you want to hang out with me?' Or, 'Don't you have other friends?' Or, 'Don't *you* have somewhere you need to be?'

This time, however, I'm able to stop the stupid questions before they're out of my mouth.

'Nothing,' I say, following him, turning my head to hide my grin.

We cross Flinders Street opposite the station, heading up Swanston Street, past the stretch that smells like fast food and horse manure. It's cruel to make those poor horses trot circles around the city all day, but to make them wait outside a Macca's and a Hungry Jack's adds insult to injury.

A little farther up, Brodie says, 'Sushi?'

I nod. He gets a box of the thumb-sized clumps of rice with little strips of raw fish on them, so pink you'd think they were artificial. I feel like I'm cheating when I get the crispy chicken and avocado. Sushi is supposed to be seafood, right? But I find seafood hard enough to stomach when it's cooked—something about them swimming where they poop.

While we're queuing to pay, I scroll through the photos of me and Matthias. Some are so embarrassing I delete them immediately. There are a few good ones.

'Did I get anything worth keeping?' Brodie asks.

For a second, I can't work out what he's asking me. But he's looking at my phone.

'Yeah, thanks for that.'

'Do you want to walk while we eat?' he asks when we've both paid.

I'm still riding a wave of blissful nervous energy after meeting Matthias—the guy who wrote *my* book—and now randomly hanging out with Brodie, so I nod, and we set off up Swanston Street. There're so many people in the city today that I keep having to sidestep to avoid bumping into them, meaning I bump into Brodie. I don't mind so much, but I don't want him thinking I'm clumsy or handsy.

'Why didn't you come with anyone today?' I feel reckless and nosy. But he shrugs and finishes his mouthful.

'My only friends who would have come had stuff on today. What about you? You're here by yourself too.'

Oh, that's right. Conversations go back and forth, don't they?

'Yeah, same, I guess. Most of my friends don't read. My best friend, Imogen, would have come, but it's her grandad's birthday.' It totally sucks Imm couldn't come. She knows how much *Things* means to me. No way I'd miss out, though. I touch my satchel to make sure the book is still there, still signed.

'Well, that worked out for me, didn't it?' Brodie says.

I gauge his face to see what he means, my mouth full of rice and chicken. My expression must be ridiculous.

'I mean, I hate eating alone.' There's a wink in his voice that makes me feel a bit weak. Maybe we should have sat down to eat.

I ask the safest question I can think of. 'What are you

reading at the moment?'

He puts the last of his little pink and white bundles in his mouth, throws the container in a bin we're passing and, while he chews, pulls a book out of his bag in answer. It's a thick fantasy book called *Each Season, the Same Changes*. I've seen it online a lot. It's pretty new and I haven't read it. But I haven't read anything much except *Things I Forgot to Say* for months.

'Is it good?' I ask.

He swallows. 'I'm only this far.' He holds the book open to his bookmark, maybe a quarter of the way in. 'But I'm enjoying it. It's warring kingdoms, but none of the main characters are royal family, so the stakes are a bit different.'

'Cool. I've always wondered what it'd be like to have a typical daily life type story, you know, school and friendships, or whatever, but set somewhere like Middle Earth.'

He laughs, and I make a note to try and make him do it more often. 'It's not like that,' he says. 'It's still battles and subterfuge. But without the obligations of royal family ties, I guess. I don't think I'm doing it justice.'

'No, I get it.'

We're at Bourke Street Mall and a tram crosses our path. People head in every direction, some with shopping bags, others backpacks or cameras. All kinds of people. I've always liked the city for that reason. Like, anyone can come here, doesn't matter who you are or if you're even planning on buying anything. Personally, I'm very used to not buying anything.

'Where do you want to go?' I ask him. I want him to make

the decisions because I don't want the responsibility. I could too easily lead us somewhere embarrassing. 'And if you need to head off, that's cool.'

He's got a disbelieving half-smile on his face as he shakes his head slightly. 'Don't worry, I've got plenty of time. Let's go this way.' He points farther up Swanston Street. 'I'll take you to one of my favourite places in the city.'

After half a block, he says, 'So tell me why *Things I Forgot to Say* means so much to you.'

It's almost a minute before I get any words out. He's basically asked me to show him the pattern of a tree's roots—I'd have to dig it all up. He'll have to appreciate the leaves and branches instead. 'Well, Cooper's family situation is similar to mine—'

He cuts in. 'Your mum's in prison?'

'No, but she left.'

'Shit, sorry. I'll shut up now. Tell it how you want.'

I choose my words carefully. 'There's a lot about Cooper that feels like me. And the whole romance with Scott, it played out exactly the same as it did with my best friend. A big mess with his parents finding out about us. He moved away at the beginning of this year and as tight as we were before, it was over.' I can feel that welling in my chest again, like every time I reread the book. Like every time I think about the past two years. Like when I squeeze the juice out of an orange and find myself identifying with the discarded skins.

'That sucks.'

'You're telling me.'

I can tell he wants to say more but is respecting my feelings. He barely knows me—some things are too raw to share, even with close friends.

We're at the lights across from the State Library. He points over the road and says, 'It's this way.'

If he takes me to the State Library, I'm going to be so disappointed. Not because it's not an amazing place, but because any book nerd worth their weight in books has been there and marvelled at the domed reading room and the galleries and things. If he thinks I don't know about it, he must think I'm pretty basic.

I'm relieved when we pass the steps and he takes me up the little street next to it. About halfway down is a bookshop. It's got a long window with an amazing display in it. Hundreds of flowers the size of grapefruits made from pages of books, with knee-high, chicken-wire people standing or sitting among them reading their own little books. It stretches all the way along the shop, for about twenty or thirty metres.

'In here,' is all he says.

We step inside and it's beautiful. There are dark wooden shelves filled with interesting leather-bound hardbacks, and an art section just begging to be browsed. We pass a coffee cart wheeled straight out of a steampunk novel and the store opens up. Everywhere your eyeballs land are antique knickknacks and displays in cabinets. Everything feels busy and curated, like we're in a museum that has been converted into a bookshop over time.

I can't believe I've never found this place. It feels like the destination of a journeying poet.

I move closer to Brodie, keeping my voice down when I speak, as if we're in a library. 'This place is amazing.'

'I know, right? I love the feeling like nearly every book here is a discovery waiting to be made.'

I've made so many discoveries today. But I still know so little about Brodie. 'What's your favourite book? Seeing you know mine.'

We're standing in the kids' section, flicking through picture books. I'm too distracted to read them properly.

'That's a tough one.'

'Not for me.'

He grins. It's wonderful. 'I know, but I've never had a book hit so close to home, I guess. It's tough because I love so many books.'

'Well, which ones have you reread?'

'I don't reread, there's too much out there.'

'Yeah, but I can't imagine not revisiting characters I've loved. It's an entirely different experience to reread. Don't you want to spend more time with people you meet and like?'

He looks at me and I feel an enormous flush blooming up my neck, a wave of heat washing over my face. I can't believe I said something like that. I wasn't aware of the double meaning until the words came out of my mouth.

'Of course I do.' He pauses. My insecurity flares. 'But it's a little different with books.'

I exhale.

We browse the shelves, pointing out books we've read and recommending them, or warning against them. There's one I point to and say how much I loved it. A gritty dystopian with a kickass pansexual girl as the lead. He takes it from the shelf and reads the back. I just recommended a pretty queer book to him and the thought that goes through my head is: *What if he's not out to his parents? I can't do that again.*

I keep waiting for him to put it back, but he holds onto it and starts talking about another book. Then we're at the front of the shop and he's handing the book over to the guy behind the counter. He's buying it on my recommendation. I'm thrilled he listened to me, but scared he won't like it. A little bit because he might think less of my recommendations in the future and a little bit because I might think less of him.

When we're back on the street I say, 'I hope you enjoy it and didn't waste your money.'

'I'm sure I will.'

'I wish I could buy more books. But our school library is pretty good.'

'The only reason I can is because I help our neighbour with her gardening and house work every week.'

'Nice set-up.'

We wander back through the city. Our conversation is easy. I tell him about Imogen, how she's as obsessed with music as I am with books. How she's always making me playlists and trying to get me into new bands or singers she's discovered. She's good, though, because she'll always give books I recommend a go.

We're being jostled down Degraves Street when it starts to rain in that instant way of Melbourne weather. We duck for cover and huddle under the eaves outside one of the cafés. We're grinning at each other in a stupid, giddy sort of way.

'Hey, let's go in here,' Brodie says as he touches my arm to lead me up the stairway entrance to a café. His touch is gentle, and I follow, wanting it to last. I can't work out if he's just being friendly or if there's more to this. Confusion can lead to getting hurt, and I'd like to think I'm done with that. What if he's straight? Thanks for nothing, universe.

The place upstairs is dimly lit and cosy. The tables are small and have tea-light candles in little coloured glass cups. The room curves around the corner, which makes me think it has heard many warm secrets. There's no one else up here and, for a moment, I wonder if it's even open.

'How's it going?' comes a voice louder than suits the little space. A woman has emerged from the back room and is smiling her welcome like a floodlight. 'What can I get you?'

I look to Brodie, as if he's going to make the decision for me but say, 'I'll have a hot chocolate.'

'Same,' he says.

'Great!' The woman's enthusiasm is overflowing. 'Take a seat and I'll bring them over.'

We take a table around the corner, out of sight from the counter. It'd be different if there were more people, but it kind of feels like we're on show, being the only ones here.

Brodie must be thinking the same thing, because he says quietly, 'She's so happy some customers came in.'

'Don't tell her we're only getting drinks.'

Even though there's a table between us, I feel like we're super close. And we're staring at each other now. It's a little bit intimidating, but I don't break away.

We don't have time to say anything else before the woman arrives with our drinks.

'Here you are, loves. Anything else?'

'No,' I say, wondering if I've got enough coins left to cover this drink.

'Can we have a plate of chips?' Brodie asks.

'Sure thing.' She disappears again.

I'm feeling a bit panicked. 'I don't have enough for chips.'

'Don't worry about it. I've got enough.'

'Are you sure?'

'Positive.'

Brodie takes a sip of his drink while I eat the froth off mine with a teaspoon—the conversation lulls. There's space for maybe twenty people in the room. But there're only two and they're not saying much right now. Face-to-face, the conversation isn't as free-flowing as it was when we were walking.

I swallow the lump in my throat. 'Hey,' I say, 'only because it's important to me, I need to ask you something.'

His eyes lock onto mine and I wonder if I'll have the courage to get it out.

'Ask away.'

I can't decide if his smile makes it easier, or harder.

'Are you into boys?'

He laughs. Loud. As loud as the woman's greeting was when we arrived. It's not the reaction I was expecting.

'Forget it,' I say, looking down into my drink and wishing I could leave.

'No, no,' his words still jump with laughter. 'I'm sorry for laughing. It's just, that question took me by surprise. Clearly, I need to up my flirting game. I've been flirting with you so hard since the signing queue.'

I glance at him again. 'Really?'

'Yes! So, yes, I'm into boys.'

I feel relief fill me up. Then I feel myself blushing again.

I somehow manage to speak. 'Cool.'

'And you are too, right?'

'My favourite book ever is *Things I Forgot to Say*. You've read it. So, you should know. But… yes.'

'You said it was important to ask. Why?'

The curtained windows dull the sound of rain outside while I try and find the right words. 'It's also from the book, I guess. Like, the rest of the title should be *Because You Didn't Think to Ask*.'

'Oh, yeah,' Brodie says. 'Like between Cooper and Scott.'

'And between Cooper and his dad.'

He nods. I can tell he gets what I'm trying to say.

'And I know everyone has their reasons one way or another,'

I say, 'but, are you out to your parents?'

He's got a thoughtful expression. 'Yeah.' He pauses for a while. 'Was it as bad as it was in the book? With "Scott's" parents?'

I shrug, trying not to let the wave of sadness come crashing back down on me. 'His parents moved away with him because they found out about us.' I've read *Things* so many times because it's like pushing on a bruise to remind you that you can feel something. 'I like to know where I stand with people. And I like people to know who they are to me.'

'Who am I to you?'

'Here you are!' The woman's loud voice cuts through and she puts a large plate of hot chips on the table between us. 'Enjoy.' And she's gone again.

She sliced right through our conversation and I don't know how to answer his question. It's probably a good thing we were interrupted—time to think.

Brodie takes a chip and bites it in half. He pushes the plate towards me, indicating I help myself.

I take one and bite into it before I realise it's too hot and have to breathe in and out a few times, juggling it inside my mouth with my tongue. When it's cool enough, I swallow and take a sip from my drink, which is only a little bit cooler, and a strange flavour mix.

Brodie has watched the whole display with an amused look on his face. I'm determined to hold his gaze.

'New,' I say. 'You're new.'

He doesn't hesitate. 'New can be good.'

'Exceptionally good,' I say, feeling more daring than I've ever felt before.

We're staring at each other, so our fingers accidentally touch when we both reach for a chip. We don't instantly pull away. It's nice.

Our conversation starts up again as easy as it was before, but there's a cosy warmth to it now, like this café, and I relax into it. I've asked the questions that were playing on my mind and now I can recognise his flirting for what it is. With the rain falling outside and us sitting in this tiny room by daytime candlelight, it's like Melbourne is cupping us in its hands.

Eventually we notice the time and I realise I should probably get going.

We go to the counter to pay, and I empty all the coins I've got in my wallet into my hand and tip it into Brodie's.

'You don't have to,' he says.

'Just take it.'

He does and pays the bill.

'Thanks, loves! Don't get too wet out there.'

We stand under the eaves on the street where we first ran from the rain. We're standing a little bit closer this time.

'I need to catch a tram from Bourke Street,' I say.

'Same. Let's cut through all the arcades.'

It's as if the people who designed Melbourne actually lived here and knew you may well need to get from one end of the CBD to the other undercover. We only have to run across the streets when the lights change. But by the time we've reached Bourke Street Mall the rain has eased right off and there are even patches of blue in the sky.

'Which tram you need?' Brodie asks.

'Ninety-six.'

'Oh my god, same!'

I can't believe we need the same tram. I start to cross over to the other side of the road but he doesn't move, so I turn and come back.

'What?'

'I've got to catch it this way, I live in St Kilda.'

'Oh, right. I go that way.' I point in the opposite direction. 'I'm in East Brunswick.'

He laughs again. It's truly a sight to see. Today has been full of sights. Matthias with his arm on my shoulder, Brodie's grin directed at me. My unicorn is frolicking.

'How epic is it we're on the same line?' His eyebrows dance lightly in amusement. He reaches into his bag. 'Take this.' He pulls out *Each Season*. 'It won't hurt to read another book.'

I stare at it.

'I can't, you haven't even finished it.'

'I've got a new book to read.' He places *Each Season* firmly in my hand. 'And it's an excuse to hang out again. Here comes my tram. Message me?'

Like there's any chance I wouldn't. 'Sure. Don't forget me among all your followers.'

'Never. I'm not Scott, remember. Call me Toby.'

With that, he's gone, running for the tram.

Toby's not necessarily a love interest for Book-Cooper. But he's a possibility. There's still the mess to deal with, but there's life after Scott.

While I wait for my tram, I post the photo of me and Matthias. This time with all the right tags. Then I pull the signed book out of my bag.

> *Dear Cooper,*
> *To be sure of others, you need to be sure of yourself.*
> *There's a beauty in you that those around you are sure to*
> *see. Don't forget to see it yourself.*
> *It was a pleasure to meet you,*
> *Matthias Brown*

I was right. I'm crying.

I look back at my phone and Matthias has already liked the photo of us. So has Brodie. My heart flutters and my tears are not tears of grief for the first time this year.

I reread what I wrote.

> **coopdegrace** Today was amazing for so many reasons! Meeting @matthiaswrites was just (a major) one of them. Shout-out to @aboymadeofbooks for the picture… and the chips.

Breathe Me In

BY

SOPHIE L MACDONALD

Take a deep breath. Close your eyes, and let it settle all around you. Smell the beery wash of the eucalyptus, and hear the constant buzzing of life from every corner. This is my world now, and it can be yours too, if you like. A place can soak through your skin like sweat, and ooze into your heart and soul. Breathe it in, and let me tell you a story.

This story steamed out of the baked soil and silvery gums and filled me up like a balloon. I'll breathe it out. You breathe it in.

We moved to Currumbudgee just after my sixteenth birthday—long enough after Dad died for Mum to start noticing me again, but not long enough for her to bear the thought of staying in London without him.

Land is cheap in Australia, if you don't mind living in the middle of nowhere. These properties stretched out in all directions: vast sprawling forests of khaki and green, tangled with undergrowth and, at the heart of it all, a shimmering creek that never seemed to moisten the soil or feed the land. Occasionally, a rainbow lorikeet or a king parrot would flash by, like an accidental splash of colour. We fell asleep to the sounds of green frogs and cicadas, and we woke to kookaburras and whipbirds.

Mum had always dreamed of travel. When I was younger, we spent summer evenings lying on oversized towels on the back lawn, waiting for the sky to darken. You don't see too many stars in London—the city lights kill it all—but we would look for the brightest star, the one that couldn't be dimmed, and Mum would squeeze my hand.

'That's our star, Mina,' she'd say. 'See it up there?'

'Do you think it's lonely?' I asked once.

'No!' She found that funny. 'It's actually surrounded by millions of friends, but we just can't see them here.' She propped herself up on her elbow and stared at me. 'One day, I'll take you somewhere we can see them. We just have to persuade Dad to come too.'

Dad never wanted to travel.

'It's a waste of money,' he would say. 'Everything we need is here.'

When he died, Mum and I moved to Australia—the land of stars. On our first night, we sat on the deck, gazing up, tears on both our faces as we pointed out the Milky Way and all the other constellations. I had never seen anything like it.

'I feel like I'm on a spaceship,' Mum whispered. 'How can there be so many stars?'

'Which one's ours?' I asked.

We both stared for a long time, before Mum answered, 'I don't know.'

~

It was Mum who introduced me to Talia. Mum was determined to meet all our new neighbours, and right here—right next door to us—found someone just for me. Maybe Talia's parents were running from something too, as she was also new to the area. It's possible the whole town was made up of grieving or lost souls. It felt our sadness—it drew us to it, I'm sure of it.

'She's from Sydney!' Mum exclaimed. 'She's the same age as you, and her mum said she doesn't know anyone here either. You'll be going to the same school next month!'

Talia was invited to come to our house for an afternoon.

I wasn't looking forward to it—those things always feel forced—but then in she walked, and I had to just stop and stare.

Talia was beautiful. She had silvery-white hair, loose around her shoulders despite the heat. Her face was small and pale, with light blue eyes that seemed almost metallic as the light caught them. I felt like a mess in the humidity, with my hair piled up and my shirt stuck to my back. She looked like an elf.

'I'm Mina,' I said, my words feeling clumsy.

'Talia,' she replied.

There was a long silence.

'Something to drink?' I said. 'Lemonade? Water?'

'No, thank you.' Talia walked straight to the window.

'Oh, do you want to go outside?' I hoped not. It was hot out there.

'I want to hear the creek,' she said.

'Okay,' I looked sideways at her, but she smiled back, so I opened the sliding doors that led outside.

She stopped me as we got to the deck, grabbing my arm, her other hand at her lips to make me quiet.

'Can you hear it?' she whispered. I must have looked blank, as she sighed and dropped my arm. 'Me neither. Not now. It gets exhausting.'

She sat on the steps of our deck, which led down to the woods—the bush—and the creek below. People owned a lot of land here, but no one looked after it. The land and all it contained just sprawled around and did what it wanted. I guess it's easier to control smaller gardens, but it also seemed to me that Australian land might not like being controlled.

'What's exhausting?' I stared down at the yard below, trying to see what she was looking at.

She glanced up at me suddenly with her intense blue eyes, and I shifted back.

'I'll tell you another time,' she said. 'When you hear it too.'

'Okay.' I wasn't sure what to say to this, so I let it be.

We sat there for some time, chatting about our old schools and what it was like to live here. It wasn't really chatting. I asked a lot of questions, and Talia gave me bland answers that didn't reveal anything.

'Have you always lived in Australia?' I said, finally, running out of things to talk about. 'It's a real change from England. I mean, it's lovely,' I added quickly in case I offended her, 'but it's a very young country. It's still developing. It doesn't have the history and the culture that we do.'

I don't know why I said it. It was stuff I'd heard Mum say to her friends. I didn't care about history or culture, except it got annoying when English friends asked if I would use a knife and fork in Australia, or if they 'even have theatre' there. I was just trying to fill the silence.

'You're wrong.' Talia stood up, her white cheeks flushed. 'That's an ignorant thing to say.'

'I'm sorry,' I said. 'I just meant it doesn't have the centuries of history that we do in England. Everything is new here. But I don't mean it as a bad thing.'

'Australia is ancient,' she said. 'Our history stretches back thousands of years—farther back than the modern England you're referring to. There are things here you don't understand—' She broke off suddenly.

'Oh, I know,' I said, keen to keep her talking. 'I know it's an old country really. Just that—' I kicked at the ground. I was insulting my first Australian friend within minutes of meeting her.

'I don't know what I'm saying,' I admitted, glancing up at her. 'I'm sorry—it's not coming across right. I can hear how awful and condescending I sound. I didn't mean to offend you. I was just making conversation. Bad conversation.' I looked down again.

'You're new here.' Talia caught my eye and smiled briefly. 'There are a lot of things you will learn.' She suddenly leant forward and took my hand. 'Australia has the oldest and most dangerous animal in the world. Do you know what it is?'

'A kind of shark?' I guessed.

She shook her head. 'A story. Let me know if you ever hear what I'm talking about.'

She was gone before I could say any more, leaving me sitting on the deck steps craning my ears for anything other than the sounds of the birds and the insects.

Later, Mum asked what I'd thought of Talia.

'She's nice,' I said carefully, 'but she's very different.'

Mum nodded, as if she had expected me to say that.

'She's had a troubled time of things,' Mum said, which told me nothing. I waited for her to go on.

'Her mum said they had to move from Sydney because Talia was having a few issues there,' Mum continued. 'I'm trusting that you won't say anything to her—' I nodded '—but it seems she got a bit obsessed with the history of the place, and she started seeing ghosts.'

Mum must have caught my expression then, because she waved a hand dismissively. 'Not real ones, obviously, but she started fixating on it. She would walk down the street and think she saw a gold miner, or a battle taking place. She started to go a bit crazy. Her mum said they had family not far from here, so she thought it made sense to move her away from the city—a new start.'

'Australia's not new,' I said, taking Talia's position automatically. 'It's ancient.'

'Well, yes, but you know what I mean,' Mum said. 'She's a

lovely girl, and her mum's hoping she'll leave that behind her now.'

'Has she?' I asked. 'Left that behind her?'

Mum paused. 'Her mum said she's not settling as well as they hoped. Maybe you can be a good friend to her. It's lovely having someone your own age next door.'

'Sure.' I nodded, slightly more enthusiastically than I felt at that point, and I tried to ignore the feeling that, despite the heat, something cold had lodged in my chest.

I woke that night, sticky with sweat, and threw myself out of bed before I even knew I was conscious.

Heart pounding, I clutched at the window ledge and looked around my room with confusion. I could hear Mum's soft snores from down the hallway, and I crept out of my room to look in at her, feeling my heart rate slow to match the rhythm of her breathing as I reassured myself that everything was normal.

I was heading back into my room when I saw her through the window.

Like a silver puddle of light in the backyard, Talia trickled down the hill towards the creek. I could just make out her hair, flashing in the moonlight between the trees as she walked.

'Talia!' I hissed, banging at the window, but she couldn't hear me. I pulled on my trainers and ran to the back door, hoping Mum wouldn't stir from her sleep.

Easing the door closed behind me, I ran out into the night.

'Talia!' I hissed it as loudly as I dared, and she stopped immediately.

Branches scratched at my ankles as I made my way down to her. I could just see the dark water of the creek below.

'What are you doing?' I grabbed her shoulder and she turned to me—pale eyes dark and blank.

I remembered reading that you should never wake a sleepwalker. I gently steered Talia back up to the deck. As I sat her down, she seemed to startle.

'Oh, I'm sorry,' I said. 'You were sleepwalking. I was worried you might go straight into the water. Are you okay?'

'I wasn't sleeping,' she said.

'Then what were you doing?' I sat next to her.

She stared at me for a long time.

'It's okay,' I said. 'You can tell me. I'm good at keeping secrets.'

'Are you really?' she asked, and I nodded vigorously. 'I wish I was.' She gave a laugh. 'Maybe we'd still be in Sydney if I'd kept my mouth shut.'

'I know a few things,' I offered, hesitantly. 'You don't have to talk about it if you don't want to. I know you—saw some things in Sydney.'

It felt like a timeless moment then—the heat, the buzz of mosquitoes, and the moon shining down on this other-worldly girl. In the middle of the night, anything is possible.

'If I tell you,' she said slowly, 'you might die.'

'If you tell me you have to kill me?' I said, with a small laugh so she didn't think I was making fun of her.

'If I tell you, then you might tell someone else, and it will just keep getting bigger and bigger. Stories can kill, you know.'

'Like a chain letter?' I asked. I had read stories about those. Pass it on or you die. Pass it on and everyone dies.

'Like a chain letter,' she repeated.

'But you have to tell someone,' I said. 'Everyone needs a friend.'

She almost laughed at that, before saying, 'I have never had a friend.'

'Talia,' I grabbed her hand, as she had mine before, 'what happened?'

'It's calling to me,' she whispered, looking down at the creek. 'Once you hear it, it means it's coming for you.' There were tears in her eyes.

'Hear what?' I was getting frustrated.

Talia tucked her feet up and faced me.

'I had visions in Sydney. If I closed my eyes, I saw everything that had happened in a place. I would see people murdering each other, as well as mundane things—people dying of old age, people shopping, people being hit by cars. I saw it all.' She closed her eyes then, as if remembering the sensation. 'It used to be something I could do when I wanted to, and I could stop it by opening my eyes, but then it started happening without me controlling it. I started to go a bit mad.' She opened her eyes suddenly. 'Well, you would, wouldn't you?'

'Yes, of course,' I said.

'Mum thought maybe stories about Sydney had crept into my head, and that if I was in a different environment I wouldn't be so crazy. She thought it was my imagination gone wild. You probably do too.'

'No, I don't,' I said, though I wasn't quite sure.

'So we moved here,' she said, waving an arm with a flourish. 'Past the black stump, as we say. Nowhere. She was right—the visions all stopped. Currumbudgee was so new and shiny and different that I couldn't possibly have crazy hallucinations here.'

We both looked out at the dark land beneath us. Nothing looked new or shiny.

'But you're still seeing things?' I asked.

'No.' Talia stopped for a moment, and pressed her hand against her mouth. 'It's worse. I can feel something waiting for me here. Something old and sleeping. Older than anything I ever saw in Sydney. A man who was working on our yard told me a story. He gave it to me, and now I'm giving it to you. Like some kind of disease, I guess.' She tried to laugh, but it came out as a sob. 'I'm sorry, Mina. I don't know if I should be happy you haven't heard it, or frightened it's only me.'

'You're not giving me anything,' I said firmly. 'What story did this man tell you?'

'It was a story he'd been told,' she said, 'about the bunyip that lives in Currumbudgee Creek.' She gestured to the bottom of the yard. 'Our creek. Your creek. It's a monster.' She leant closer. 'It's huge, with a head like a crocodile, feathers on its body, and walrus tusks. It winds through the creek like a snake, and it has a horse's tail. It's always hungry, and always looking for food. It eats humans, and if you ever hear it howl then it is coming for you.'

'Why would he tell you that?' I shook my head. 'Was he trying to scare you?'

'He was frightened,' Talia said. 'He told me he'd started to hear the howls. It had woken him up at night, and he'd felt compelled to walk down to the water. He managed to run before he got right to the edge, but he was afraid that one night it would get him and drag him under.'

'You can't believe that.' I said it flatly, punctuating it with a slap at a mosquito on my leg. I glanced to the house, hoping Mum was still asleep. 'What did you say it was? A bunyip?'

'It's an ancient legend,' said Talia. 'People have feared bunyips for centuries.' She shook her head. 'We are new here, but we are in an old place.'

'So it's just a myth?' I asked. 'Like the Loch Ness Monster?'

'Kind of,' Talia said, 'but, for centuries, people all over the country have reported seeing or hearing them. Explorers even found a skull once.'

'You've heard these howls?' I asked, and she nodded. 'But why do you go outside then? If it lives in the creek, why not just stay inside?'

'I can't.' Talia's shoulders sagged. 'It's awful, Mina. The worst sound you could imagine—like a devil calling you. You can't help but go. There's a little girl who goes down there all the time—I tried telling her it wasn't safe, but she ignored me.'

'She comes in the garden?' I asked.

Talia nodded. 'It's not really a garden, is it?' We both looked out at the acreage below us: dark, sprawling, endless. 'I think her house backs onto our land, and she comes to play in the creek. She shouldn't do it.'

'Have you told your mum about any of this?' I asked.

'No.' Talia shook her head. 'She thinks I'm crazy anyway. Also, I don't want to put her in danger. There's something about this story—it feels like a curse to pass it on. When the storyteller dies, whoever heard their story begins to hear the howls.'

We stared at each other, and the night air seemed suddenly cold.

'It's like it's hungry,' she continued, 'and it gets into your head, and you have to tell people about it.'

For a moment I imagined a reflection of the creek swimming through her eyes. The air felt thick on my lungs and I began to cough.

'If you hear it, I'm sorry.' Talia got up and walked quickly towards the gate at the side of our land. 'Take care, Mina,' she said.

I didn't see Talia the following day. Mum took me into town on errands, and we weren't home before sunset. Talia's story had played on my mind, but it seemed ridiculous under blue skies and hot sun. Several times I opened my mouth to tell Mum, but superstition kept me from saying anything.

I don't want to put her in danger.

I stayed awake for as long as possible that night. I left my window cracked open a little, so I might hear her footsteps outside, but when I opened my eyes it was morning, and the smell of coffee drifted down the hall. I dressed quickly.

'I might go to Talia's today,' I said.

'Great!' Mum said. 'I'll drive you there.'

'Oh, you don't have to,' I said quickly. 'There's a gate joining the two blocks from the back. I can just go in that way.'

'I don't think you should just turn up in her garden like that.' Mum frowned. 'I'll call her mother and check.'

Mum went to make the call, and I poured myself a coffee. An uneasy feeling was drifting through me like a dark cloud. I shook my shoulders and legs. Ridiculous.

'Mina, come here, please.' Mum's voice was urgent. She was on the phone to Talia's mum. 'Did Talia say anything to you about sneaking out last night?'

'No,' I said.

'Think hard, Mina.' Mum spoke sharply. 'Any boyfriends? Anyone she might have wanted to see?'

'No,' I whispered, 'but the night before, she was in our garden. She was walking to the creek.'

'What?' Mum stared at me for a moment, before repeating it to Talia's mum. 'What was she doing?' Mum asked.

The seconds stretched out between us.

'Sleepwalking.' My mouth was dry. 'I think she was sleepwalking.'

Mum finished her phone call and tried to ask more questions, but I had nothing more to say. Shortly afterwards, there was a knock at the door, and Mum opened it to find a police officer wanting to speak to me.

As Mum hovered in the background, the police officer—a tall young man who introduced himself as Coen—asked me about my relationship with Talia.

'I didn't really know her,' I said.

'Were you friends?'

'I've only just moved here.' I glanced up at Mum.

'Talia was a troubled girl,' Mum informed him. 'Mina was kind to her, but I don't think they were friends.'

'In what way would you say she was troubled?' Coen asked me.

'She was just a bit different.' I shrugged. 'She talked about ghosts and things.'

'Tell me more about these things,' he said.

'Her mother will tell you,' Mum said. 'They moved here because of it. I think she has some sort of mental illness.'

'She's not ill,' I said. 'I don't know anything apart from that and the sleepwalking.' I could feel sweat forming around my hairline. Coen leaned in.

'Did Talia report hearing or seeing anything unusual to you? Did she hear any strange noises?'

'Mina?' Mum nudged me. 'Answer the question.'

The air felt thick. My lungs were filling with the sticky humid air, and I glanced out to the backyard.

Something waiting. Something ancient.

'No,' I said. 'I didn't know her.'

Coen looked at me for a long time, but I tried to fix my gaze on the trees outside. So still. I couldn't even hear the birds. It was as if the whole outside was waiting for me. I held my breath.

'Mina, if you think of anything, please call me.' He handed me a card. 'If you hear anything strange—' he gave me a pointed look '—you can talk to me.' He nodded to the backyard. 'My parents live near the back of your block. I think my little sister, Kirra, comes to play in the creek sometimes. If you ever see her, make sure you stop and say hello. She can tell you a lot about this area.'

I nodded, clinging to the table, and let Mum show him out. My head was spinning. He knew. Talia's story was true.

As soon as he had gone, Mum came and put her arms around me. She cried for a long time. She told me it was in sympathy with Talia's mum, but I think she was crying for Dad. Our star had friends here in this hot country's night sky, but we had no one.

The police searched the creek. It wasn't deep, and they walked the length of it, but they didn't find anything. As I watched from our deck, all I could think was that the winding line of the creek looked like a brown serpent slithering through the trees. Perhaps it had a crocodile's head. Perhaps it had a horse's tail.

At night-time I asked to sleep in Mum's bed.

'Of course,' she said, and held me like she did when I was little. 'Talia had a lot of problems, Mina. I shouldn't have encouraged you to befriend her. We'll just have to hope that she's found safely.'

'I didn't really know her,' I said.

'Did I do the right thing?' Mum said suddenly. 'Bringing us here?'

'Of course you did.' I pulled back in surprise. 'You always wanted to go somewhere new. See something different.'

'Everywhere ends up being the same, though,' she said. 'As long as there are people around, it's all the same.'

I didn't know what to say, and I thought she was asleep for a moment, but then she mumbled something.

'I think Dad must be having the greatest adventure of all,' she said, 'and the worst part is that he's the one who never wanted to see anything.' She gave a short bark of a laugh and pulled me close. 'Goodnight, Mina.'

I cuddled close to her, safe in the warmth of her body and her sounds. Sleep didn't come easily, but eventually I felt myself drift away.

I dreamt of Talia. I saw her lying in the creek, surrounded by flowers, like poor Ophelia from *Hamlet*. Her white-blonde hair was shimmering across the surface of the water but, as I watched, it started turning into thousands of tiny feathers. Her arms and legs became flippers, and a horse's tail spread underneath her. Her face began to elongate and lengthen, and her body stretched, until she had a snake's body and the face of a crocodile. Huge tusks ripped through her cheeks, and she opened her mouth and began to howl.

I awoke with a scream, sheets damp with sweat. Mum did not stir.

I took a deep breath, thinking of mundane things to calm my mind—a trick I had used as a child. Maths homework. Making a sandwich.

I crouched beneath the covers as the noise came again—a terrible howl that wrapped around my head and made my stomach clench. It was coming from the backyard. It was calling me.

My legs swung out of bed and began to move me towards the back door. I fought to stay in bed and, when that failed, I tried to drop to the floor—but my body would not obey me. I slowly walked down the path towards the creek.

The hot night air clung to my face like a veil. The smell of eucalyptus filled my nose. I desperately tried to scream and break away, but my body kept walking towards the water. The creek looked black and cool and, for a moment, I imagined plunging in and swimming deeper than was possible—down into a bottomless sea, where silence and stillness would wash over me forever.

'You're not dreaming.'

A voice cut through the howls, and I dropped to my knees on the rocks.

A little girl was crouched by the water.

'I see you all come here,' she said. 'You crazy people. You

come to die.' She laughed.

The noise had stopped, and the creek looked small again—gently flowing through the darkness. All I could hear were frogs.

'I'm Kirra,' she said, 'and you are a crazy lady who thinks she wants to die.'

'Kirra,' I repeated. Her pyjamas were dotted with purple stars. 'I met your brother.'

'I know,' she said. 'The bunyip took the other lady.'

'Talia?'

'The lady with the long white hair.' She laughed again. 'I told her not to come here. She was worried about me, but she didn't know I am safe.'

'Why are you safe?' I moved back from the water.

'Because I won't do what it wants.' She shrugged. 'My family has been here forever. We know all the stories. We know when to talk and when to be quiet.'

'Is it a curse?' I asked. 'Now I've heard it—does that mean I'm going to die too?'

'Probably,' she said, with another shrug.

I tried to steady my breathing, but the air was so heavy it felt like I was drowning on land.

'Is there a way to stop it? Can I fight it?' I pictured the creature from my nightmare.

'No.' Kirra shook her head. 'The bunyip is very strong. It is made up of every person it has ever taken. When it gets you, you become part of it forever. You can't fight the bunyip. It is a very bad devil.'

'So what do I do?' I asked.

'Go to bed,' said Kirra. 'Don't tell. It wants you to tell. The more people who believe in it, the bigger it gets.'

'I won't tell.' I stood up. 'Thank you for saving me. Please be careful here. You should go home to bed now. Do your parents know you come here at night?'

'Don't worry about me,' she said. 'Maybe see you later, if you don't die.'

I left her there by the creek and went back to my own bed where, despite the heat, I wrapped myself up in my quilt.

Mum was busy the next day, and she left me home alone, which gave me time to think. I watched the clock anxiously, counting down until sunset, when the bunyip would return.

I went through all that I knew from what Talia and Kirra had told me. The bunyip was a creature—a monster of sorts. It was made up of everyone it had taken, and it needed people to believe in it and talk about it. Stories helped it spread from one person to another, like an infection. If you told someone about it, you had done what it needed, and it would consume you and seek them out next. *Stories can kill you.*

So, what if I didn't tell anyone? What if, like Kirra's family, I never told anyone about the legend or about the howls? Would that be enough to save me?

I found the card that Coen had given me, and dialled the number. He picked up immediately.

'Coen, it's Mina—the girl from—'

'Hi, Mina.' He cut me off. 'I hear you saw my sister last night.'

'Yes. She helped me.'

'Do you need any more help, Mina?' he asked.

'Yes.' I didn't know what help he could give. 'The bunyip—' I felt ridiculous saying it during the daytime.

'Don't talk about it to anyone else,' he said immediately. 'There are things that have left my family alone, because we don't talk about them. I will tell Kirra to look out for you again tonight.'

'Is she safe out there at night?' I asked. 'She's so little. What if she fell in?'

'She's fine,' he said. 'She's safer out there than you are.'

'Did you find Talia?' I asked.

'That's between the police and her family,' he said. 'I can't discuss that with you.'

'But you know it took her,' I said.

'We create our future with stories from the past, Mina.' His voice was quiet. 'Be careful which stories you choose to tell, and which you choose to conceal.'

Night crept in and, despite my fear, sleep came quickly. It was as if a black blanket had been dropped over my head, and I couldn't stay awake.

I was immediately underwater. I tried to turn and pull myself out, but instead I felt my lungs filling as I clawed to rise to the surface.

My lungs were burning, and little stars were exploding in front of my eyes. I tried to tell myself I was still in my bed, asleep, but I wasn't so sure. What if I had already walked down to the water's edge without realising? I was drowning.

The bunyip's howl was all around me, and I felt it as a gut-wrenching pull in the base of my stomach. As the monster circled me, I let out a scream of my own.

'What do you want?' The words flowed out of my mouth and through the water like little strings of jewels. 'You want stories? I can write stories about you. Please don't kill me. If you let me go, I will tell everyone my story, and the whole world will know about you.'

It seemed to be waiting.

'I'm the last one, aren't I?' I continued. 'I haven't told anyone else, so if you kill me then your story ends here—which means you die too. You know Kirra's family will never tell. I'm all you have.'

The howl had stopped, and I could hear nothing but the sound of water hitting the rocks. The bunyip's eyes dulled, and its tail dropped.

'Aren't you tired of all these people who just confide in one other person?' I asked. 'Weren't you once a great legend? I can make you a legend again. I promise I will help you.'

The bunyip turned its long snout to the side, teeth shining in the water. It blinked once, and then shot away from me, leaving a huge wake behind it.

The water threw me. I landed on hands and knees next to

the creek, where I coughed and spluttered and cried.

I sank back onto my haunches. The creek was once again shallow, and I could see the dark shape of the rocks at the bottom. Impossible for me to have been so far underwater there. I looked up at the house. Had I done it? Had I struck a deal with the monster? Was I safe?

'You're a stupid lady.' Kirra was looking at me from the opposite bank, shaking her head. This time she was wearing pink pyjamas and a fluffy dressing gown. 'I tell you "don't tell", but you promise the bunyip you will tell everyone. What do you think will happen? You're killing a lot of people.'

'I don't know,' I said. 'I tried to give it what it wanted. Maybe if I only tell people in England then it can't get to them.'

'The bunyip can come through any water,' Kirra said. 'Any water anywhere. You make it famous, it will have a very big dinner.'

Her words took a moment to sink in.

'If I don't tell anyone, it starves,' I said, 'but it will come for me first.'

She shrugged. 'You will make the right choice,' she said. 'I am not coming back here again. If you go to the bunyip tomorrow night, I will not save you.'

Before I could respond, she had disappeared into the darkness and, with Kirra gone, I suddenly felt afraid. I ran back up to the house full speed, until I hit someone and sent both of us flying.

'Mum!' I crouched at her side. 'What are you doing here?'

Mum took a moment to register me.

'I thought I heard something,' she said slowly. 'Why are you outside? Why are you wet?'

A low moan crept through me, and it took a moment to realise I was the one making the noise.

'Did you hear the howls?' I said urgently. 'How did you know? Did someone tell you?'

'Talia's mum told me the police found her diary,' Mum said. 'Full of rubbish about curses and legends.'

I stared at her for a moment, afraid that with any words I said, my fear and grief would fall out of my mouth and bury us both.

'I could've sworn I heard something,' she said. 'Maybe it was just a dream.'

'Just a dream,' I echoed.

'The creek's pretty at night,' Mum said wistfully. 'Look at the stars reflected in it. It's like looking at a sky you can touch.' She reached a hand towards it, and I grabbed her.

'Let's go in,' I said. 'Back to bed. Come on.'

I led her back to bed, and she fell asleep immediately, a small smile on her face.

Early in the morning, I sat at the edge of the creek and trailed my hand in the water.

'I know you're in there,' I said. 'I want to talk to you.'

Beads of sweat snaked down my back and my chest. The insects had paused, and a water dragon crouched, staring at me from the other side of the creek. The sky was such a bright blue that it didn't look real. I focused on the dark water below me.

I leant forward until my hair trailed in the water. The reflection of my face stared back at me, and I saw the creek mirrored back and forth to infinity.

I breathed in and kept leaning forward, passing softly through the surface of the water. I floated down and down, impossibly deep, and the cool water filled my mouth. I couldn't see the beast, but I knew it must be there.

Waiting. Watching.

'I want to make a different deal with you,' I said, the words passing like silvery fish from my mouth. 'But first you need to promise to leave my mother alone.'

The water stirred around me, but still the bunyip did not emerge.

'You take people into you,' I said, 'so maybe people can take you out of here too. I will take a part of you with me when I leave here, and you can walk with me—wherever I go—for as long as I live, but you can't feed on anyone. I will sustain you. I will keep you alive, but you must not hunt for as long as you are on land.'

I held out my hand. 'You can come with me. You can make sure your stories are heard.'

The bunyip's face was on mine, and I closed my eyes. I felt its hot breath swirling through the water and I breathed it in.

'Mina, there's no going back.'

I opened my eyes to see Talia, floating like a mermaid in front of me.

'We can't come out of the water,' she said, 'but you can stay.'

Before I could reply, there came a muffled shout from above the water—Mum was there at the surface, calling my name.

I opened my mouth to shout back, to tell her to stay where she was, but then her hand reached down towards me and, without thinking, I grabbed it and she floated down with me.

She drifted silently underwater, eyes wide, staring at me and then Talia.

'How is this possible?' she said.

'I wrote a story,' Talia replied. 'I tried to see things from the bunyip's point of view, and I realised how lonely it must be to be a legend—a dying mystical thing—in a world where people either know you're there but won't acknowledge you, or don't believe you're there at all.

'The bunyip deserves its legend. It deserves its stories. Don't we all want to be known and remembered? Stories give this beast its breath and its life. At the heart of Australia is the oldest story of them all, and it flows through everything.'

She took both our hands in hers.

'I don't think the bunyip will come after every person who reads my diary. I think it wants to be remembered, and I think if it knows that people believe in it, it won't need to keep hunting for the next storyteller. I knew it was coming for me, Mina. I want to be remembered too.'

I looked to Mum, but she had the same dreamy smile I had

seen the night before.

'We all want to be remembered,' she said. 'Tell me, Talia, what do the stars look like from underneath the water?'

'They're beautiful.' Talia smiled back. 'I feel as if I'm in a spaceship swimming through them. It's so peaceful here, and there is no loneliness. We are all here together. Mum will be with me soon.'

'That's the bunyip talking,' I said. 'This isn't how you really feel, Talia. You've just become a part of it and now you want to infect everyone else with it too.' I tried to pull my hand away, but Mum and Talia held on.

'What an adventure,' Mum said. 'To be immortalised as a legend forever—never to lose the ones you love. Think about it, Mina, we could swim through the starlight together forever.'

'You're both thinking like the bunyip,' I said. 'We need to get out of the water.' I kicked my legs hard but could not rise up to the surface.

'Just relax,' Talia advised. 'Close your eyes, and let it settle all around you. Breathe it in.'

I clung to Mum, and we breathed the water in, and the stories of a million years swam through our veins. A feeling of peace flowed through me, and I could once again hear the birds calling from above the water. Mum and I smiled at each other.

'An adventure,' she said.

'An adventure,' I agreed.

We swam as one, me, Mum, Talia, and countless souls, in a

joyful dance through the water.

'Are we it?' I whispered. 'Are we the bunyip?'

Talia nodded. 'Wait for night-time,' she said. 'We are a dragon, shooting through the stars. There is nothing like it.'

I let out a laugh, but the noise that echoed from the creek sounded like a howl.

Stories can kill, but stories must be told. If legends are forgotten, then who knows what monsters will appear to fill the gaps? There is no fear in this story anymore. Come and see for yourself.

I'll breathe it out. You breathe it in.

Remnants

BY
KM STAMER-SQUAIR

Florida is underwater. Shanghai continues to choke on the world's mess, its skyscrapers left standing like magnificent monuments. Half of Tokyo's urban sprawl lies crumbling beneath impenetrable fog. The infected and the injured—bird, dog, rat, human—are cowering beneath the fortifications of the elite.

Here is the world, drowning in rubbish.

Clots of landfill scattered over every line on every map.

I remember the old days, but I remember them through other people. Or through written words, or traces of memories. I collect the history of what was, and try to imagine it into the what is. The Old Days don't exist anymore. Back then, the seasons were shorter and the weather was milder and the food tasted better—although not everyone had it, not even then. There were more animals but fewer human animals, and more colours, too—particularly green. Particularly blue. Cold and hot existed but there were happy mediums as well, like spring afternoons and summer showers, or the smearing of pastel colours during the sunrise.

Not like today.

I chew on these stories as I hear them, and try to focus them into existence, as if it's possible to digest the past in order to feed a future. I like the sound of this middle ground. I want to taste it.

These days, the grey areas have seeped through all the cracks in the hard, barren earth, and all we've got left are extremes: the black and the white. Flood. Drought. Burning sun. Violent storms. No life, or too much of it. Daytime. Night-time.

Sleep. Awaken. Repeat. The world sits, blanketed in debris, struggling to breathe.

This will hopefully be a nice story.

Grandma zips up her suit and gives me one last kiss, although with her purifier on there's no real physical contact, it's more a bop of the head. She doesn't look at Dave before she leaves, because Dave never approves. The whole process is short and routine.

'Stay safe,' Aunty Gina says, her usual farewell. Her hair is coming loose from its bun, strands sticking to her neck. She's been close to the surface already today, working all morning at the compost, sorting out plastic and metal scraps that have been gleaned from dumpsites up above. Hot work. Dirty. The heat of the sun cooks the air through the ceiling of rock, so it's always humid, what with the hundreds of bodies crammed into such a tight space.

Grandma acknowledges this—and dismisses it—with a brisk nod, and then winks at me. I'm always the last one she winks at before she ascends.

Ascending is considered risky business, especially during the light of day. Children are banned from doing it without parental accompaniment and, even then, it has to be for a special reason. No one ventures out onto the surface while the sun is up unless they have to. Even with our suits and purifiers, we hear stories from others about those who go missing, those who must have suffocated or dehydrated or come out badly against a spliced animal. Some may have just burnt, despite their layers. Fried by the UV, like an egg.

Grandma ascends quite regularly. She's considered odd for that. It used to be only so often, maybe once a month or so, and only when there was new information, or a new idea or a new hope, and someone needed to check it out. Back in her younger days, she studied in a field called 'biochemistry'. It's how she and my grandpa met. When Grandpa died two years ago, Grandma started ascending more regularly. I think she misses him less when she's out there, somehow. I don't understand it. This is all speculation.

Grandma exits via the valve with her back to us, so all I can see is her white suit and her white travel pack strapped into place. As soon as the red light above the valve winks back to yellow, signifying that the cylinder is empty once more, we resume our usual activities.

No one really monitors who comes and goes in our encampment, not anymore. Only the nutters want to get out, view the plains from a goldfish tank. The officials don't care who takes risks, so long as people are only gambling with their own lives. If their palm print checks out and they're over eighteen—and new people aren't coming *in*—then it's all fair game.

I watch the others trickle away. It's just like every other time we watch Grandma leave and say goodbye. Dave makes no noise except a slight grunt in his throat as he returns to the latrines. My family retreats, burrowing back into their underground nooks, trying not to worry about Grandma because 'you can't waste time worrying about everyone'.

Speculation. Imagination. So many metres above my head, my grandmother touches the earth, body frozen beneath an awakened sun.

I find it difficult to picture.

So many noises—voices, footsteps, music—clutter the landscape. The earth no longer breathes with the tides but asphyxiates to the oppressive sound of humankind. Sirens blare in the distance. Endless streams of cars and engines create an impenetrable thrum-thrum *on clogged freeways, churning out blackish smog, smudging out the sky. Impatience, excitement, despair, joy: the synchronicity of expression, the rising crescendo of chaos. Silence has lost its meaning. Lights shine everywhere. Billions of artificial flares, beaming without a break. The stars must still exist out there, but does anyone bother to look up and check?*

My days are split between my duties and endless free time. Somewhere over in the east side, informal classes have started up, but they're not mandatory and I don't think my family likes the idea of me travelling that far. What is there to learn, anyway, that isn't hidden in the past?

I collect stories from the mouths of old ones and patch them together during my morning shifts cleaning equipment at the kitchens. While I sanitise and reseal the shiny metal tubes of Chlorophyll—tasteless, but high in nutrients and easily grown, so why complain when at least we're fed?—I try to mentally catalogue the tales. It's hard to keep track of so many words, especially when they convey such foreign concepts. But I don't have any paper, so my memory is all I've got.

Here in Australia, all of us live underground. Or at least, those of us who escaped the cyclones up north do. It's not terrible—we're not like the poor souls in Mumbai or Bangkok—but I've heard there are small pockets of the earth where people still live outside, can still feel sunlight on their skin, so long as they bathe regularly in anti-UV cream.

I'm nostalgic for times that preceded and surpassed me. I want the stories imprinted on my future.

I used to share these stories with my friend, Siti, before she left. We grew up in neighbouring segments, and our duty shifts overlapped. I would finish packing distribution kits just as Siti would arrive for cleaning duty. Talking is restricted during commute times because of the noise and the amount of people that flood the halls. Most people sign or lip read. But Siti and I would meet up after her shift and make rude mockeries of our duty leaders. We were young, and we didn't have much else to do, so it didn't take long for us to bond.

'When I grow up,' she would say, sitting cross-legged on the ground, 'I'm going to be a communicator.'

After just sharing what I'd heard that morning about the old communicators—the hoards, the billions, who could send instantaneous messages and codes to anyone ready to receive them—I was in awe of this idea too. While communicators rarely used the web to interface anymore (too many encryptions, too much hacking, nothing was safe, what were other countries plotting with it?) it was still considered an aspirational job. Only those with the highest level of clearance graduated to communications. Tracking and monitoring information, relaying messages to foreign settlements; tasks like these were shrouded in mystery. Common folk weren't told much about what was going on in the encampment, much less about what was going on above their own heads. Grandma told me it was so nobody would panic. My mum seemed angry at her for having said that; she pursed her lips and ended our discussion. But I still remember it.

Siti found these stories interesting, like I did. The youngest of seven children, she liked to dream about a certain kind of freedom. When she left—back when you *could* leave, when they were still allowing a select few to go and search for family members who were masked in silence overseas—I stopped being able to talk so freely to anyone but Grandma. Old Times talk was seemingly reserved for those who had experienced it, the ones whose eyes had been open to the world once, and therefore had reason to miss it.

'It's silly to waste so much time talking about it,' Dave would say to me, stepping out of his boots so they could be sanitised. 'It's futile—the past just gets people depressed.' Working in the latrines was never very pretty, but he didn't appear to mind so much.

I try to like Dave, I really do. He's my cousin, Aunty Gina's oldest. He's sharp as a tack and can make anything with his hands from anything, so long as he can't find a reason why he doesn't want to.

I love him, I guess. I just get frustrated by the things he says. Mum says it's because we're both too stubborn. Grandma said it was because I like to dream, and Dave is afraid to.

Plastic bottles. Fishing wire. Broken dreams. Forty-six thousand acres of e-waste form Ghana's landscape along the Korle Lagoon. Nothing left but trash. Hundreds of scavengers who spend hours sifting through wires and plugs and cords and dead devices, a sea of dead bodies, of hard metal shells. Shipments roll in from the UK, from Australia, from Hong Kong, places hunting for more space. But there isn't any. There are more products produced every minute than there are humans, so where does it all go? Into the dump, skyward bound, a one-way ticket to disaster. Meanwhile—

Stop. There is nowhere for it to go.

'Melody.'

Someone says my name in such a way that I hear it for the first time.

Melody.

My eyes open in the dark, but I can't see anything except the distant glow of the solar-powered orb above. I've fallen asleep in the communal room by mistake—it's obvious that it's past light-out.

I go to sit up, groggy. There is someone crouched next to me.

'Melody,' they say again, and I realise it's Aunty Gina. Her voice sounds strange.

'What is it?' I whisper, aware that our whole segment is likely asleep. I can't sign; there's not enough light to see by.

Aunty Gina makes almost no noise as she leans towards me to press her lips against my ear. Her breath vibrates as she mouths the words: *Grandma isn't back yet.*

Electricity crackles along my cheek.

I follow her out of the room, hurrying. We know the layout of our segment so well that we make almost no sound. At the end of one of the main passages is the ascension dock, where I said goodbye to Grandma earlier that day. Or was it yesterday? We have no concept of time outside light-on and light-off and the regularity of our shifts. It's not as concrete as it used to be, not important.

My family is at the ascension dock when I arrive. We're unusually large for an intact family; not many survived so whole. Even so, the room feels empty and cold. The light above the ascension pod is dead, just as we all are. Inanimate. Silent. Filled with dread.

Dave breaks first. Of course.

'This is just the sort of thing—'

'Hush,' Aunty Gina says to him, taking a quiet step towards the others.

'There's no point worrying yet…' Tom, my mother's brother-in-law, is often the mediator. He always keeps a calm head.

I notice then that not all of my family is in the room, after all. The young ones haven't been woken, and although my gut is clenched tight, I feel a small surge of pride when I realise I'm the youngest one there, the only child among adults. I've been chosen to participate in this conversation. I cling to this thought, refusing to notice any others.

'Maybe she got lost,' my mother murmurs. She wears her usual brown smock; clearly, she never changed into her sleepwear. Her fingers worry the stone around her neck, the stone from my dad, from a different life.

'Or just lost track of time,' Tom suggests.

It's a quiet conversation, pressed in between the walls of the earth. Being awake after light-out isn't an unsanctioned activity, but it's an offence to make an audible disturbance, and the soundproofing in our zone is dodgy, always has been. Not that noise is an issue right now; everyone's voices seem choked by anxiety. Grandma should have been back long ago.

I watch their faces, wondering what will be done. It's too early yet to alert the authorities, but if she's not back within the two-day shift, it will be too late to do anything at all.

'So what should we do?' Dave asks the blank room. We're all empty spaces. 'Did she say anything to anyone before she left?'

The whole episode is a whisper, a secret shoved in between a dream. I think of Grandma's face, and her white suit, and her glow above the red earth.

Do we ever really say what needs to be said?

China's economic collapse results in the deaths of some ninety-four thousand people and triggers the strikes—the first ones. Barrels of protesters screaming, fists clawed, pictures on the news (if they still have the news) of bodies and faces and fear. Whole swarms of people, buried beneath their own waste. Russia happens next, then India. Is this the beginning of the end?

Of course not: there is no end.

Some start to bury their heads in the sand and go underground, lucky ones try (more die) fleeing. People reach out to relatives in Sweden or Iceland or anyplace they think might stand a chance, but the world is one place, there's no escaping it.

The acid rain continues to pollute the soil, while in Borneo, the last orang-utan dies.

Look down, below.

A whole species, crawling: as (in)significant as ants.

'Come here,' my mother says to me, taking me into her arms.

It's midway through her shift; she's going to get a strike on her record for being absent. She holds me together for a moment, her scent filling every one of my cells. The stone around her neck presses into the invisible space between our bodies. I try not to think, and just breathe.

Once upon a time, my grandma was a young girl who lived upon the surface of the earth with myriad other things. She studied at institutes called 'universities' and freely rode aeroplanes to different countries for holidays and ate a bounty of different food each day, living the rainbow, the full spectrum of colour. Garbage was thrown away in dumpsters and transported to mystical, invisible places and waste was flushed or buried or swallowed up, never to be thought of again. The skies were hazy with pollution and the waters poisoned with plastic but none of this touched her life that much, not where she lived, not then. I know not everyone lived like this—that people and places and other beings were swept into the margins, where they lurked amongst the shadows, waiting to be noticed. But I like to imagine that they all did. I like to envision a peaceful cooperation. An acknowledged interdependence.

My mother releases me from her chest but her hands stay on me, connected. She pulls me towards the valve and carefully reaches towards the white suits, bringing me one. I stare at her, questions in my eyes.

'Why...?' I try to say, but that seems enough.

She smiles at me sadly, pulling my body along, helping me get the white sheath on, like I'm little again and getting dressed for the next shift. She dons a similar one, larger in size, just as shiny. I know what is happening and where we are going.

I know that she knows—she's guessed, or just come to realise, like I did. I just don't know *why*.

'It's time, isn't it,' is all she says, hooking up my purifier. Her fingers work on the screen. The light flicks red. Ready. Awake. She pulls me into the dock with her, arm around me. I'm drowning in her touch.

It takes less time than I remember, getting to the surface. The last time I was outside was during a full moon, when I was nine, maybe ten. I barely have time to think, to process. What part of the day is it right now?

It's warmer when we reach the top room. There is only one small window, a small sliver of outside peering in. My mother guides me out the dome, away from the grey and the equipment and the dark, but pretty soon her arms fall away from me and I'm untethered, free. I hardly know what to do with what I see.

Light spills onto the dusty ground, refracted all around me. Dazzling.

Hot.

The heat creates waves in the distance, ripples of air. Barren, but breathing. Is that really the sun I see, mellow above the empty horizon? Even through my insulated layers, it tickles my skin.

Huge.

Life.

There are no trees, there's nothing but the flat landscape and smoggy sky and a bleeding disk of light. But it's alive.

It's beautiful. I can't breathe.

I love it.

My mother has faded into the distance. I'm not aware of anything except the immensity of space. I'm living the live-feed of memories fed to me through generations.

We can't speak with our equipment on, and it takes my mother's touch on my arm for me to turn and see she's trying to point something out to me. There, on the opposite side of the sky, rests the moon. The sun and the moon, still coexisting, side by side.

Late afternoon. Unfathomable.

I've strayed from the encampment, the underground maze of my life, without even realising it. The top room sits in the distance, the gateway to an insignificant world. I'm drunk on light and space. My mother is a white shadow, trailing me. I think I finally understand. I think this moment, out here, was the one that fuelled my grandma's story.

We sit on the earth. The panel on my wrist blinks its steady red beep. Grandma's dead, or soon will be. I can't be angry at her, even when I'm sad. I can only try to understand.

Here upon the land, creatures of the world. The Earth keeps spinning and the days keep coming and a bigger narrative eclipses these moments.

It outlives us all.

Mediocre Heroes

BY

SARAH TAVIANI

'So I've been working really hard to improve my speed with high-intensity interval training? You know, HIIT? And I feel like I could be getting my powers soon? Any week now, you know?'

Harrison had a habit of making all his sentences sound like questions. Harrison was also a bit blurry around the edges, so unless I'd accidentally ordered a magic mushroom risotto for lunch, he was going to be invisible by the end of the session. We all kept exchanging glances but no one said a thing in case Harrison freaked out and solidified again accidentally.

Our group leader, Micah, turned to me. 'How about you, Nat? How have you been pushing yourself this week?'

'Well, I—'

The door banged open. 'Shit,' someone said.

We all swivelled in our seats to stare at the girl in the entryway. She had dark skin and the shiniest hair I'd ever seen. She was wearing a polka-dot skirt and a pastel-green button-up shirt that should've made her look sweet and innocent, but there was something about her eyeliner that suggested she could beat you in a fight. You don't get a cat-eye that sharp without a certain scary amount of determination.

'Sorry,' the girl said, slightly out of breath. 'Am I in the right place?'

'This is the support group, if that's what you're looking for,' Micah said warmly.

'Great.' The girl headed for the spare chair next to me. As she slid into place, her bag dropped to the ground with a loud thump. 'Sorry,' she said again, wincing.

'Nat is just about to tell us about her week,' Micah said, gesturing to me. 'We'll let you settle in and then you can introduce yourself.'

The girl grinned and pulled a bottle of water from her bag, taking a long swig.

'How are you feeling this week?' Micah asked, tearing my gaze away from the new girl.

'Fine,' I said. 'Super. I mean, not *super*-super, but I had that big fundraiser at my old high school this week to repair the gym and it went well. We got a lot of donations and everyone said they had a great time. Which made me feel…' I trailed off, trying to find the words. It was always a little uncomfortable baring your soul with new people in the room.

'I guess it's good that there are other things in my life that can make me feel happy and fulfilled,' I finished, a little louder than I intended.

'It's not an exact science,' Micah said soothingly, brushing his lanky brown hair behind his ears. 'We have no idea how this generation's powers will manifest, and you may just be someone who develops a lot later in life.'

'I know that,' I said flatly. We'd been over this so many times. 'It's just… I'm turning nineteen in a few weeks and everyone else's powers came in during puberty or a little after. Maybe once you hit a certain age and your powers haven't come in, you automatically get the power of a spinster aunt or something. Maybe I'll become like a homing beacon for cats.'

The girl next to me giggled but stopped immediately when she realised no one else was laughing. I think it was supposed to be a friendly, encouraging laugh, but I felt my cheeks flush with embarrassment all the same.

'Anyway, that's it,' I said. 'That was my week.'

'Thank you for sharing, Nat,' Micah said, and the sentiment was echoed a second later by a dozen droning voices from around the circle.

We all turned to the new girl, who had caught her breath and was looking significantly less frazzled.

'Hi, everyone,' she said, arcing her hand in a neat wave. 'I'm Amina. Sorry I was late. I have to say that the public transport here is *hopeless*.'

'Must be a good day, then,' I said. Amina grinned at me.

'I'm eighteen, like Nat, and I haven't had any of the usual symptoms,' Amina continued. 'No incredible strength or invisibility or sudden x-ray vision that allows me to see into the girls' change rooms when I walk past. This is my first time at, like, a government-run support group but a few of my friends were in the same boat so we all leaned on each other. I just moved here for uni, so I'm really glad I found this group. Who knows? Maybe a change of scenery is all I need to get my powers going. That'd be a nice surprise.'

'Thank you for sharing, Amina,' we all said.

There were only a few people left in the circle, and no new developments. Everyone was keeping one eye on Harrison's progress, some with unveiled envy, others with quiet interest.

'Does he know it's happening?' Amina whispered to me.

'Not a clue,' I murmured back. 'He thinks he's about to become the fastest man alive.'

'Sucks,' she said sympathetically.

I blinked, taken aback. I was so used to wanting any kind of power that I never thought what it would be like to get something like Harrison's. Not all invisibility could be turned off and on; this might be the last time we saw him.

The meeting wrapped up and the group headed straight for the cake and biscuits, but I wasn't up for socialising. Most of the people my age had come and gone a long time ago, and the chasm between me and the others in the group was widening exponentially. Some of them hadn't even started high school.

I managed to spot Harrison's shirt floating through the crowd. I hugged him awkwardly, trying to track his movements by the faint outlines of his arms.

'I'm really proud of you, buddy,' I said.

'I'm telling you, it's the HIIT?' he said. 'I spent ages focusing on cross-country—'

'Look in the mirror, you dork,' I said. I tried to ruffle his hair and ended up accidentally smacking him in the face, so I decided that was my cue.

As I was heading out, Amina grabbed my arm.

'Are you catching the bus?' she asked. 'Can we walk together?'

'Sure,' I said automatically. 'Actually, I don't know why I said that. I drove, but I can give you a lift home.'

'Really? I live over in the new subdivision. That's not too far, is it?'

'Not at all,' I lied, glad I'd filled up my car.

Amina was easy to talk to. We were starting at the same university the next week, and both majoring in sociology, which gave me a little thrill. Outside the support group, it could be hard to strike up a conversation with people.

I mean, it's not like being powerless is a *disease* but a person's superpower is that automatic ice-breaker they can rely on when meeting someone new. When you explain that you don't have any powers, there's always an awkward pause as the other person works out whether to apologise or pretend they didn't hear you. As if you just told them you're grieving the loss of a family member. I'm sure they don't do it intentionally, but I've seen less disgusted expressions when someone takes off their shoes and socks during a flight.

'You said you've been going for six years?' Amina said, as I sailed through another intersection. 'How many people have, y'know, levelled up?'

'I've lost count,' I said, before realising it was another lie.

'Forty-three, including Harrison.'

'Jeez.' She sat back in her seat, quiet for a moment. 'That must be rough.'

'I'd like to say it gets easier, but…' I trailed off with a shrug.

'I used to think that if I could just fly, everything would be fine,' Amina said. 'Then if I could just levitate, it would be fine. If I could just jump really high, it would be fine. If I could just do this, if I could just do that. At this point, I'd be happy with even the most mediocre power. Like, if I could just do the perfect cat-eye or always pick a perfectly-ripe avocado, I would be ecstatic.'

'Or if you could afford avocado *and* a house deposit?' I suggested.

'Exactly.'

'Although they'd probably hit you with the Super Tax if you ever let on about the avocados. And then you can say goodbye to that house.'

The drive to Amina's house was quicker than I expected. At this time of day, the roads should've been blocked but I was on the best green-light run of my life. Still, I felt like I'd spent hours in Amina's company, and there was a pang of regret when we said our goodbyes and she hopped out of the car.

'Hey,' I called after her, winding down the window. She turned towards me, shielding her eyes against the light drizzle of rain. 'Your cat-eye is already pretty perfect.'

She laughed again and waved. Amina was generous with her smiles and laughs, whether out of nerves or because she was just a generally happy person. But I still felt like I'd won a small victory when I said or did something to bring them about. I couldn't remember the last time I'd made a friend my own age who wasn't already a super.

I drove slowly out of the subdivision, trying to savour the happy buzz, but the light turned green and I left Amina behind.

No one is quite sure when the first superpowers started manifesting; the first case may not have even been reported. All the action films in the world can't prepare you for the terrifying moment when your own life gets turned upside down. Or so I've been told, anyway.

Everyone's pretty sure about the *why*, though. Let's just say big companies shouldn't be playing with chemicals they don't understand. And they definitely shouldn't be letting them spill everywhere like a kids' chemistry set. But that's most adults for you, I guess. Just keep doing something dangerous because weapons are more important than actual safety, and keep going until it all blows up in your face. Then blame someone else. Sounds like a plan.

The adults were the first ones with superpowers. Flying. Invisibility. Laser vision. Super hearing. And since it's something you can't control or stop, the government decided the best way to deal with it was to impose a new 'Super Tax'. Fortunately for the government, of all the new powers that manifested, no one was blessed with the ability to outrun the Tax Office.

When the supers started popping out babies, it was a whole

big thing. Some of the parents-to-be got reality shows, some were hounded by paparazzi, and most of them were scared out of their wits. Who knew if they could even carry the babies to term? Who knew if the mothers and babies would survive labour? Who knew what kind of lifespan the babies would be looking at, with all these new chemicals in their systems?

Turns out they were just like any other births. Mostly. One woman with heat vision accidentally burnt a hole in the side of a building when her contractions started but that's what the Super Tax is for.

They called us the Super Generation. Like we were going to change the world from the moment we first drew breath. The thing is, most of us didn't show any signs of superpowers right at the start. Some got their powers quite young, but most had to wait until puberty hit. And some, like me, were still waiting.

The support group was for members of the Super Generation whose powers had yet to develop. It was kind of a crappy situation, because when someone stopped turning up it meant that they'd gotten their powers. And they were always too busy to stop by and say, 'Hey, here's the secret.'

Super is the new normal.

For the longest time, I thought it was a coincidence. It was Amina who pointed out that something strange was going on.

'This only ever happens when I'm with you,' she said, as I drove her home from uni one day. 'Otherwise, I get the worst luck with traffic lights. I'm always stuck for ages.'

I laughed it off as a quirk. I was like one of those people who could always fluke a parking spot right outside the entrance to the shops, or someone who happened to fast-forward through ads on TV to the exact right moment.

Then I started putting it to the test. Every single time I came to a traffic light, it would turn green and I would move on, sometimes to the screeching of brakes and exasperated yells of other drivers. It didn't matter whether I was a pedestrian or a driver, whether the lights were on a timer or a sensor. I tried sprinting up to a pedestrian crossing to see if my speed could confuse it. I found deserted streets and tried slamming my foot on the accelerator. As soon as I got within two metres of the nearest traffic light, it changed.

After six weeks, I figured I had to report it. I rocked up to the local Super Department and took a number, scrolling through my phone as I watched people walk up to the counters and demonstrate their superpowers. Most of the younger kids were excited, probably because they didn't understand how much the Super Tax would siphon from their pay slips in the future.

People in their teens were looking more hostile about the whole situation. Most of them were probably already working casual jobs around uni and school, so the Super Tax hit hard. And for some people—the ones who had abilities that would be useful in reconnaissance or combat—registering as a super meant they were automatically enlisted in the army and required to go wherever the Department saw fit.

As I was flicking through an ancient copy of *Women's Weekly*, one girl started screaming about the injustice of being forced to move to Townsville in her final year of high school. She crushed three chairs with her bare hands before security escorted her out of the building, tranquiliser guns at the ready if she broke loose.

Finally, my number flashed on the screen and I was instructed to go to counter 13.

'WelcometotheSuperDepartmentthanksforwaitingmyname isMargarethowcanIhelpyou?' the woman behind the counter sighed in one breath.

'Hi, Margaret. I need to register my abilities,' I said, unable to stop a little flutter in my stomach. This was it. It was finally happening.

'Active or passive ability?'

'Passive,' I said, handing over my forms.

Margaret scanned the form and paused, then looked up at me with one eyebrow arched over the rim of her glasses. 'Honey, how old are you?'

'Nineteen.'

'Do you understand the penalties for submitting a fraudulent Super Declaration?'

'Yes, but I'm not—'

'You're telling me that your ability is turning traffic lights green?'

'Yes.'

'I'm not sure how you expect me to lodge that. Super

abilities must be assessed at a registry counter within the Department. If you can't show me your ability right now, then it doesn't exist.'

'I have plenty of documentation and footage,' I said, pulling a USB out of my bag. 'It's all on there.'

'As video footage can be tampered with, it is not an accepted form of demonstration under the Super Tax Act.'

'Are you kidding me? How do you assess the people who can breathe underwater?'

'Buckets,' Margaret grunted.

'Look, if you just come with me for five minutes—'

'No can do,' Margaret said. 'Sorry, but you're just going to have to accept that you don't have any abilities.'

'But I *do*,' I protested. 'Seriously, any traffic light, *anywhere*. Pedestrian or driving.'

'That does not fall into any of the recognised power categories stipulated in section 2A of the Super Tax Act,' Margaret said. 'You can apply for an independent examination if you believe you've been wrongfully turned away.'

'Great,' I said, relieved. 'I'll do that, then. How do I apply for that?'

'You fill out these forms.' She slapped a book on the counter. It was thicker than some of my uni textbooks. 'There's a two-year waitlist.'

'Look,' I said, clearing my throat and trying on my best understanding smile. 'I'm not psyched to be signing up for another tax, but I'm trying to be honest with you guys.'

'I don't deal in honesty,' Margaret said. 'I deal in forms. Fill out the appropriate ones and come back.'

'Did you hear what you just said?'

'Fill out these forms,' she repeated, 'and come back.'

'Fine,' I said, grabbing the book and walking off. I knew my ability would sound stupid to some people, but that didn't mean it wasn't real. I bet *Margaret* would recognise it as an ability the next time she was stuck in a two-hour traffic jam.

I tried to find other people like me. I put ads up at uni and spread the word on Facebook. I even wrote in to a news website with a story idea and their article went viral. I set up an email address for people to contact me, and hate mail flooded in from both sides—supers who thought I was looking for attention, and regulars who'd decided I thought myself above them.

The few cases that seemed legit turned out to be from tin-hat conspiracy theorists or people who wanted me to send nudes. After a few weeks, I stopped responding to anyone. After a few months, I stopped reading the emails altogether.

Finally, I came clean to the support group, and was met with silence. Amina reached over and grabbed my hand, but no one else said a thing.

And then, 'So you have powers now?'

It was Chelsea, a thirteen-year-old blonde girl who'd been coming for a few weeks.

'Well, not according to the government,' I said. 'But

Amina's seen them. It's like—'

'I don't get why you're complaining,' Chelsea interrupted.

I started. 'Excuse me?'

'We're all sitting around, waiting for our powers to manifest, and you're complaining that yours aren't *super enough*?'

I took a deep breath. 'Chelsea, you're thirteen—'

'It's Emily,' she said harshly.

'Sorry,' I said. '*Emily*, you're thirteen. You've only just started going through puberty. Your powers are probably going to show up any week now.'

'Hey now,' Micah said.

'Easy for you to say,' Emily muttered.

'Not *easy for me to say*,' I snarled. 'Try waiting another six years with nothing and then being told you're not good enough. That who you are is never going to be good enough. You want to do that and then get back to me?'

'But you got your powers, right?' Emily said, looking bored as she twirled a strand of hair around her finger. 'So what are you still doing here?'

I felt a lump form in my throat. 'I wanted some support,' I said quietly.

'The people here want support because we might never have what you have,' Emily said. 'You don't belong here anymore.'

'Are you freaking kidding me?'

'Hey now,' Micah said.

'No,' said Emily. 'I'm not "freaking kidding" you. You're just taking up space now. We have *real* problems, much bigger than you having to fill out forms, and you're trying to make this all about you.'

'It's a group sharing session,' I pointed out. 'I just took my turn.'

'You shouldn't *get* a turn,' Emily yelled.

'Hey now,' Micah said.

'Really?' I said, rounding on Micah. 'I've been in this group for nearly seven years and all you have to say is "hey now"?'

'This is not about taking sides,' Micah said. 'You have a point, and so does Emily.'

Emily sat back in her chair, smirking like she'd won. Which I guess she had. Even Micah didn't seem to think that I belonged here anymore.

'You know what?' I grabbed my bag and stood up, knocking over my chair in the process. 'I'm leaving. Anna is right—'

'It's Emily.'

'People have real problems, Nicole,' I shouted at her. 'Bigger than me getting your damn name right. And you know what, Michelle? I hope that if you ever get powers like mine, Rachel, that you go through this exact thing and realise what an absolute fucking *bitch* you were being.'

'*Natalie*,' Micah said.

'Hey now,' I said, pointing my finger at him. 'I'm leaving the group, so you don't get to tell me how to act.'

'That was extreme,' Amina said at lunch the next day. 'I mean, I liked it. But it was extreme.'

'I probably shouldn't have gotten that riled up,' I said, my forehead pressed into the table. 'She's only thirteen.'

'You were right, though,' Amina said. 'I caught her telling one of the other girls that she'd never develop superpowers if she didn't lose ten kilos because "fat people never get powers and that's just science". Sometimes thirteen-year-olds can be bitches.'

'Okay, I feel less bad,' I said, sitting up. A serviette was stuck to my head and I slapped it back down on the table.

'Look on the bright side,' Amina said. 'You don't have to pay that stupid tax and you can get wherever you want to go faster than anyone else. And by "look on the bright side" I mean that I literally cannot find a downside to this.'

'I just wanted recognition,' I told her. 'I just wanted that little stamp on my license. My family threw a huge party when my cousin started breathing fire, but they're never going to believe me about this. They're just so elitist. They've all had stereotypical powers and anyone who doesn't fit the mould isn't going to cut it. My nonna doesn't even have powers and she's already embarrassed by me because she thinks I'm letting down the gene pool. "Natalie, you never marry if you no have powers. No man want woman without powers."'

'Well, screw your nonna.'

'Ew.'

'I'm serious,' Amina laughed. 'You know the truth and I know the truth, and anyone who spends any time around you is going to know the truth. So what if your family thinks it's just good luck or a phase? Do they really need to know?'

'No,' I said, gloomily shovelling the food around my plate. 'I just would've liked to make them proud of me.'

'You can make them proud of you in other ways,' Amina said, handing me a flyer. 'How about we go to this together? You said your family was struggling with the Super Tax, right?'

I looked at the flyer. Another 'Stop the Super Tax' march was being held in the city over the weekend.

'I don't know,' I sighed. 'I mean, I should probably go because I know that I'm part of that community, but I just don't feel like I belong there. Everyone's going to be showing off their powers. That one guy is going to be playing hopscotch with skyscrapers like he does at every march, just so he can make the joke about leaping tall buildings in a single bound, and what am I going to be doing? Quietly turning traffic lights green? The street's already going to be shut down for the march, so I will be zero help.'

Amina bit her lip. 'The march isn't just about showing off powers. You know that, right? It's about solidarity and standing up for what you believe in. Do you believe in equality for supers or don't you?'

'Of course I do.'

'Then *go*, Nat,' Amina said. 'Besides, it's not like the people who can breathe underwater are going to be wheeled through the streets in fish tanks to prove a point.'

'There's a first time for everything.'

Amina took a deep breath and started packing up her

things, shoving textbooks into her bag a little harder than was necessary.

'Woah, woah,' I said, frowning. 'What's the matter?'

'I just…' Amina cleared her throat. 'You're my best friend. I love you no matter what. But I don't like this attitude. You've been brooding for weeks over something that actually doesn't make your life any harder—'

'That's not—'

'—logistically speaking,' Amina said louder, drowning out my objection. 'I'm happy that you've discovered your power, Nat, I really am. But since this whole thing started, it's all we've talked about. You've never once asked me how I feel about the fact that I still don't have any powers at all.'

'We talk about that stuff at support group,' I said weakly, feeling my throat constrict. I hated this conversation. I wanted it to stop. But a niggling voice told me that Amina was right; I honestly couldn't remember the last conversation we'd had that wasn't about me.

'I want to be your friend, Nat,' Amina said. 'Not your acquaintance from support group. Just every so often I want to talk about something other than you and your powers.'

'Okay,' I said slowly. 'Um, what are you doing for the assignment in—'

'Not now,' Amina groaned. 'I can't—I have a headache and I want to go home.'

'I'll drive you,' I said, standing with Amina.

'No,' she said, holding up her hands. 'I need a break for

today, okay? And I think you do too. Just… I don't know. Think about it. You have powers, but that doesn't define you. It doesn't have to be the only thing in your life worth mentioning.'

I sat in front of my computer that night, hair still wet from the shower, eyes still red from the self-indulgent cry I'd allowed myself. I was about to delete the email account I'd set up for people to contact me. I hadn't checked it for nearly four months, hadn't even thought about it, but people were still writing in.

One person was writing regularly, too. Someone called Archie Stevens, with the subject line *RE: Proof.* Probably another conspiracy theorist.

I selected all the emails and trashed them. I was about to shut down the account altogether when another email from Archie arrived.

Sorry for bugging you, the email snippet read, *but I finally caught…* My mouse hovered over the trash icon for a second before I sighed and clicked on Archie's message.

… I finally caught it on camera and I thought you might like to see what I'm talking about. I know it's stupid but what else do you call something like this?

There was a link below, and I hoped that my antivirus software was up to date. Then a private YouTube video loaded, and someone was speaking. '—get it to focus,' the voice said.

The camera was facing a kitchen table, and a boy with shocking red hair and freckle-streaked skin walked backwards, squinting at the camera.

'Hi,' the boy said. 'My name's Archie, and I'm a Mediocre Hero.' He cringed. 'That sounded so stupid. This had better work now that there's a camera on me.'

Archie reached out of frame and picked up a box of Oreos, upending it on the table. The biscuits rolled around in circles before settling in a pile. Then Archie swiped his hand across the stack as if to knock it off the table and onto the floor.

Except that didn't happen.

The biscuits bounced back just at the edge of the table, refusing to fall. Archie looked at the camera.

'Did you see that?'

As he swiped his hand back and forth, I put the video on full screen and watched the biscuits bounce up and down, side to side, spin wildly to avoid the edge of the table.

Not one crumb fell.

'It's any kind of food,' he said. 'I can still knock over a glass or something, just not food. But that's… I guess that's my power. Stopping crumbs from falling. It's… yeah, I don't know how I feel about it, but I don't have to vacuum as much these days.'

'What are you doing? Can I have one?' A voice said from off-screen, and a boy of about twelve walked in and grabbed an Oreo off the table. I squinted and watched as a small trail of crumbs fell from his hands.

Archie walked towards the camera and switched it off.

~

It's been a year since I found Archie. Or since Archie found me, I guess. It took a while, but we tracked down others like us: a dude who's like a human ring light and takes the best selfies I've ever seen; a girl who never loses Wi-Fi, no matter where she is; people who act like actual compasses and can always find their way, but only in department stores and shopping centres; people who can always predict what happens next on TV shows, right down to the dialogue and inflection.

Even though we found each other and could talk about our experiences, it all kind of faded into the background. Once we stopped treating our friendship like a support group, it was like this weight had been lifted from all of us. We spent more time watching movies, going to trivia nights, and trying out escape rooms than we did talking about our powers.

I shouldn't be surprised that Amina was right; she's always been smarter than me.

And it turns out Amina's a regular super. She started levitating in her sleep a few months ago. It didn't help that she'd fallen asleep on the couch after we'd watched *The Exorcist*. I've never screamed so loudly in my life.

Most people still don't believe us. They think we're blips on the radar of the Super Generation; those kids who never got powers and can't let it go. And maybe we are. Maybe it's all in our heads. But if this is what being mediocre means, I'm pretty damn happy with it.

Take that, Margaret.

The Swan

BY

FELICITY MARTIN

Marlowe was crying. She hadn't meant to, but the moment she'd reached the edge of the reed-lined lake she had collapsed, and the dam had burst. For what felt like hours, she sobbed the heartbroken sobs of a girl whose whole world was ending. When she finally ran out of tears, the sun was setting, casting the wetlands in a dim twilight. Above Marlowe's head, the stars were winking into existence one by one. Orion, the most familiar and comforting constellation to her, sparked high above. Instinctively, she searched through tear-blurred eyes for his belt—a habit she had developed years ago during family camping trips, before she grew up and realised she hated camping.

At this time of year, the day clung desperately to the world, and Marlowe knew it would be twilight for a long time. Her hands had become sticky from wiping at the ropes of snot that flowed from her nose and over her chin. Marlowe was an ugly crier.

I should wash my face, she thought.

As she shuffled down to the water, she became aware of someone watching her. No, not someone, some*thing*. The prickling at the back of her neck didn't subside when Marlowe looked up and saw a black swan staring at her. It was almost invisible against the darkening lake but for the bright, ruby-red slash of its beak. She maintained eye contact with the bird as she splashed her hands and face with bronze water that was the same temperature as the tepid air around her. The swan watched her the entire time, unblinking and unmoving.

It was not quiet or peaceful here in the wetlands; the screaming of cicadas and the calling of frogs bored its way into Marlowe's skull. She couldn't think, but that was a good thing. Apart from one word, her mind was empty. One word that broke free and echoed the cicada's cries, so that it seemed like the whole world was screaming the same thing: *hopeless, hopeless, hopeless*. It was inescapable. Her body recoiled at the sound, curling inward as if to protect her heart. Only when she nearly fell did she realise that she was shaking violently and couldn't stop.

Then, suddenly, underneath it all was a new sound. A hissing that grew louder and louder until Marlowe was forced back and back through the mud and away from the lake. The sound was loud enough to drown everything else out. The swan waded and waddled its way slowly up the bank, its baleful glare still fixed on Marlowe. She could not tear her eyes away. She tripped on a mangrove root and went sprawling in the mud. For a moment there was silence. Not just the quiet heartbeat of a summer night, but true, deafening silence.

And then the swan screamed.

With a rush of wings its huge black bulk was airborne. It

passed over Marlowe, its feathers brushing her face in the barest of whispers, before it disappeared into the night.

Marlowe ran the whole way home.

When she woke in the morning, the sun was hot and glaring, and Marlowe hoped the night before had all been a dream. A strange dream, but a dream nonetheless. She sat up and barely smothered a scream. The swan sat at the end of her bed, a blotch of darkness in the bright room. The loud ticking of her clock echoed around the room as Marlowe stared at the intruder. Her mother knocked at the door and Marlowe sent her away.

'I'll be up in a minute!' she grumbled.

Marlowe scooted slowly to the edge of her bed and, when the swan didn't respond, swung her legs over the side. The second she put her weight on the balls of her feet, the bird lashed out, biting the arm closest to it. Marlowe recoiled and cried out. It had been a small bite, but blood welled up between her fingers—much too red in the early morning light—and tears sprang, unbidden, in Marlowe's eyes. She needed to get a band-aid, but they were in the bathroom. She tried three times to get up and to the door, but each time, she barely took a single step before the swan attacked. Finally, defeated, Marlowe sank to the floor and curled up beside her bed. She hurt all over. There was no way she was going to make it out the door today.

She spent the day in her room with the swan, only leaving to shuffle to the bathroom, the swan waddling behind her like a shadow. The purple-black circles under her eyes helped Marlowe convince her mother that she was too ill to go to her morning lectures, too sick to do anything but curl up, unmoving, on her bed, watching the swan with eyes as liquid and red as its own. As night fell, the swan ducked its head beneath a wing. Taking this as cue that she was finally allowed to move, Marlowe stood up. Immediately, her vision went black and she swayed, slumping back down on the bed as a wave of nausea crashed over her.

She had done nothing all day and it had been exhausting. She wanted to eat, but when her mother obligingly brought her some toast, the food stuck in her throat and turned her stomach further. Her mother looked at her through eyes narrowed with worry but left her to sleep—after all, sleep was supposed to be the great healer of ills.

Marlowe lay heavy and stiff as a log in her bed—the mattress too soft, the blankets too suffocating, even the presence of her tiny stuffed frog, Gerald, was too much. The swan pressed its weight into her calves, heavy and hot in the close, humid air. It was as if the swan was trying to absorb her into itself. Finally, *finally*, Marlowe slipped away into sleep only to wake again, unable to breathe, the swan's ember-bright eyes an inch away from hers. She tried to shift the thing, but her fingers slid on its soft feathers, unable to gain a purchase. Finally, she gave up and, gasping and exhausted, watched the dawn creep across her bedroom. It wasn't until her alarm rang at 6.30 a.m. that the swan slowly inched its way down to the end of the bed.

Warily, Marlowe pushed herself upright. She watched the swan as she carefully put one foot down and then the other. The swan didn't even blink. She was so tired it took every effort to move, but without the swan weighing her down, even that felt like practically no effort at all. It did not move as she opened the door, though when she later climbed out of a scalding hot shower, it was sitting on the pile of clean towels by the sink. It simply watched with its unblinking eyes as she dried herself.

The swan did nothing but watch her all day. Marlowe did not see it move but whenever she glanced out of the corner of her eye it was there—on the dining table as she made toast, in the backseat of her car as she drove to uni, in her lecture halls and tutorials—though it did nothing but make its presence known, fixing her with its burning gaze and sending chills up and down her spine. Marlowe held her breath, waiting for it to strike, but her fears were unfounded. This went on the next day, and the next, and the next, until Marlowe began to think that the first day had simply been an anomaly, that the black swan that haunted her every movement was just a new pet she had somehow picked up.

Then it was Saturday, and Marlowe had a party in the evening. Her best friend's friend had invited her, and it was expected to be a standard house party with lots of people crowding in the kitchen, all of them talking over one another, little food and lots of alcohol. Marlowe had been looking forward to it. She was hoping for a meaningless make-out or two, maybe even something more if she could swing it. She hoped she would be able to hide the swan from everyone as well as she hid it from her family. Explaining a large, coal-black swan to a bunch of drunken bogans would be difficult at best.

Marlowe had all day until she had to get ready, and she spent much of it reading. Upon moving to get up, however, she was being held down by the heavy bulk of the swan. When had that happened? She poked it with a finger.

'Move,' she ordered. It just ruffled its feathers and glared at her. 'C'mon, not this again, I have places to be.' The swan didn't move. When Marlowe pushed it again it bit the inside of her wrist.

'No no no no no no.' Marlowe tried to hold back tears but they spilled all too easily from her eyes as she sucked at her oozing wrist. She glared at the swan on her lap. How dare this… this thing keep her from her life. It filled her with a rage that stuck in her throat and made her gag. Before she knew what she was doing, she struck it with her book. It made a satisfying thwack, so she did it again and again and again.

The swan did not respond. It did not react as she threw the book aside and used her own bare hands to beat and claw at the silent thing, pulling oily black feathers free of its wings and wringing its delicate neck.

Finally, panting and spitting feathers from her grinning teeth, her fingernails torn and bleeding, Marlowe stood triumphant over the battered corpse of the black swan that had haunted her for a week. She grinned as she stepped over it and cleaned herself up. She grinned as she dressed for the party, met up with her friends, and drank and danced and flirted.

Marlowe was having the time of her life and couldn't get enough. A cute Asian girl with spiky hair pulled her into the shadows and kissed her. Marlowe fell in love with her a little bit. She spent the rest of the night glued to the girl's side, smiling a softly pleased smile. The girl let Marlowe rest her chin on the top of her head, making the both of them laugh.

For an instant, the crowd parted and Marlowe stiffened. Trance-like, she moved through the crowd to the other side of the room. She faintly heard the girl call out to her but the sound went unheeded. Every one of her senses was focused on one thing—the night-black swan perched on the end of the stair banister. With a light touch, she stroked its perfectly formed head and sinuous neck. Its feathers were soft and glossy and unmarred by gore. Marvelling at its very existence, Marlowe picked it up. It was heavy and all too real in her embrace. She could feel its heartbeat resonating with her own, and for a moment, she loved this perfect thing. Gently cradling the swan in her arms, she left the party without a word. She hadn't gotten the cute girl's number.

Marlowe slowly grew used to the swan's eternal presence. Day and night it was there. Sometimes it held her down in the middle of the night and she woke up panting and gasping for air. More often, however, it simply sat, and watched, and waited. To keep it at bay, Marlowe would feed it her own blood from her chest, like a perverse *Madonna and Child*. Occasionally, the swan demanded more of her, eating into her flesh, but mostly it was satiated with what she willingly gave. Yet, eventually, Marlowe couldn't imagine her life without her swan in it. She would say goodnight to the world and sit up in bed with a cup of tea and the swan on her lap, and would wonder at the way the light glistened on its feathers like petroleum, how the thing was simultaneously the most beautiful and most terrifying thing she had ever seen.

Marlowe met a girl at university and they fell in love. The swan disappeared for a while; Marlowe wasn't sure if she missed it. Her grades rose and she went out more often, but underneath it all remained a lingering fear and a desire for her swan to return. Without realising, it had become a part of her—as much as she loathed the thing it turned her into, she didn't know who she was without it. After living this way for a year or so, Marlowe and her girlfriend decided to move in together.

One day, the swan came back. All Marlowe's revulsion for this intruder returned in a wave. 'Why are you here?' she yelled at it. 'What do you want from me?'

Tears streamed from her eyes and she wrapped her arms around herself as if to let go would be to let herself fall apart. She was glad her girlfriend was at work over the Christmas holidays. Glad there was no one to see her like this.

Marlowe screamed and swore at the swan but it remained impassive. The longer the swan stared at her, the more enraged Marlowe became.

'I hate you,' she sobbed, collapsing next to it. 'I wish you would die.'

As always, the swan said nothing back. It did not move as she wrapped her arms around it and cried into its oily wings.

Slowly, her sadness died, replaced by a frenzied restlessness and the need to do something, anything. Marlowe held the swan's wings pinioned to its sides, even though she knew it would not struggle, and threw it in the oven. The acrid scent of charred feathers and the sweet smell of poultry flesh filled the sweltering apartment, nauseating her. After an hour, Marlowe pulled it out again and set it on the dining table where she had laid out silver cutlery and the fine china she had inherited from her grandmother. She ate the whole bird down to the bones, which she then broke open to suck out the marrow. Mouthful after mouthful stuck in her throat and made her gag but she pressed on. She ate and ate but was not sated.

Marlowe became a vegetarian that day and could not abide the smell of meat ever again. Her girlfriend couldn't stand the change.

'It's like you've suddenly become a completely different person,' she said. She moved out the week after. Marlowe had plenty of company, however, as the swan spent every night curled up with her.

Rubbish piled up in the halls, dishes in the kitchen. The swan would hold Marlowe down for days at a time, letting her up for work if she was very, very lucky, but mostly she had to call in sick. She was never hungry and would feed the swan her own dinner. Unappeased, the gluttonous creature ate a hollow spot into her stomach just above her right hip, but she woke up whole—Prometheus and his eagle had nothing on Marlowe and her swan.

Marlowe woke to springtime sunrise and the soft *loo-loo-la-loo* of a lonely magpie. Something had to change. The swan allowed her to shift its body just enough for her to stand and make her way to the bathroom, where she picked up her razor. She kept her eyes locked on the swan as her long, brown locks fell one by one to the ground. She fed them to the swan and felt lighter. It slept at the end of her bed that night. The next day, Marlowe pushed open the door to her apartment and waded through an avalanching mountain of junk mail. She didn't go far, only to the local shops to buy ingredients for dinner, but it was *something*.

On the walk home, the bottom of her grocery bag broke.

'No, no, nonononono…' Marlowe muttered, holding back tears. *I finally go outside…* She gathered up the food within reach and held it close to her body as if it were the most precious thing in the world. Oily black wings brushed her cheek, just out of sight, and for a moment the whole world trembled. Marlowe was afraid to let go even to reach for the oranges that had rolled farther away. She didn't have to. As she watched, a hand reached down and picked one of them up before holding it out to her. Marlowe looked up into the eyes of a familiar face. She was older, and her hair was long, rather than spiky, but Marlowe remembered her. The woman smiled down at her and Marlowe felt a wave of warmth flood through her, strengthening her. She accepted both the orange and the outstretched hand, and climbed to her feet.

'Hey, I think we met at a party a few years ago,' the woman said. 'Marlowe, right?'

Marlowe winced as she remembered the woman was friends with a boy she no longer talked to. Sometimes that's how life went.

'Would you like to get a drink sometime?' the woman asked.

Marlowe smiled.

'I would love to.'

This time, she got the cute girl's phone number.

The cute girl's name was Alia, and she was an ornithologist. Marlowe spent their first few dates in a state of abject terror, certain that Alia would find the swan and Marlowe would be revealed as the fraud she was. After a year of hiding the swan from Alia's searching gaze, Marlowe realised that, like all the others, she was not able to see it, ornithologist or no. What Alia could easily see, however, was the effect the swan had on Marlowe.

'There's something you're not telling me, and it's keeping us apart.' Alia looked at Marlowe pointedly over the half-unpacked boxes strewn around their newish apartment. Marlowe had known this day was coming. Her secrecy had been the source of numerous fights between them, but for some reason, Alia had stayed. Marlowe took a long time to respond, weighing up her options and trying not to shrink under her girlfriend's scrutiny. Finally, she took a deep, steadying breath and told Alia about the first time she had seen the swan, and how it had haunted her ever since. The story broke from her like a wave, a cathartic release of pent-up feeling.

'Swans don't drink blood,' Alia said when Marlowe was finally silent.

'What?' Marlowe could only stare in surprise; she had expected almost any other reaction.

'It's not good for them, and it's clearly not good for you. Greens like spinach, or even a little bit of rice would be better.'

Marlowe looked at her through narrowed eyes. 'This isn't your problem to fix, you know. I was doing just fine before you.'

'Were you?' Alia merely cocked an eyebrow, leaving Marlowe to duck her head in embarrassment as she mumbled her reply.

'Not really.'

'You don't owe it any part of yourself,' Alia urged.

'But it *is* me, I don't know who I would be without it!'

'You'd be amazing.'

Marlowe shattered. Sobs racked her body and Alia just held her, quiet and still, unaware of the hissing swan mere feet away. Unaware that at this moment her presence was all that held Marlowe down to the earth.

The next morning, Marlowe snuck out and bought some spinach. Hesitantly, she held a leaf out to the swan, who only eyed it with disdain before snipping at the inside of her elbow.

Tears dripped from her eyes in love and failure as, resigned, Marlowe gathered the swan in her arms and held it close. The following day, she tried again, with the same result. The day after that was more successful; she threw a handful of leaves to the swan rather than going to it herself. The swan didn't move, but when Marlowe came back later the spinach was gone, and the swan didn't come any closer to her.

Over the next few weeks she succeeded again and again, her resolve growing stronger with each success. After she fed the swan, it would keep its distance, no longer waking Marlowe in the middle of the night, or holding her down when she had to go out. Until, one day, without warning, it wouldn't let her move. Marlowe fed it everything she had and still it wouldn't budge.

Alia was distraught at Marlowe's backslide, and Marlowe doubly so to see her girlfriend so upset. Then, two days later, everything was normal again. The swan accepted a few rice grains and kept away, though not out of sight. Marlowe couldn't look at it for fear the spell would break and it would come for her again.

That evening, Alia sat Marlowe down on their couch.

She's going to break up with me, Marlowe thought, instinctively reaching for her swan—her only constant companion in life.

'Will you marry me?' Alia said.

The swan remained with Marlowe for the rest of her life. Sometimes it went away for months or years at a time, but it always came back. As she grew older, Marlowe loved it less, hated it less. She accepted it and would welcome it back into her life like an old acquaintance, but not as a friend or an enemy. Sometimes, however, she couldn't let go of their shared history and, late at night, she would hold the swan close, long after Alia had gone to sleep. But every morning she would try and let it go again.

When Marlowe was very old, she sat up one night to listen to the song of crickets while her wife slept quietly beside her. It was a warm night and she lost herself in thoughts of long ago. She looked up as the swan flew in through the open window on whisper-quiet wings. A sense of peace flooded through her as it settled onto her lap.

She remembered when she first met the swan, and marvelled that she had ever been so afraid. Marlowe glanced down at her hands with their frail skin like crumpled paper. She never could have imagined having hands like these all those years ago.

Marlowe smiled.

'I won, you know,' she said softly, and the swan dipped its head—the only acknowledgment she had ever seen it make. 'I won.'

The Chinese Menu for the Afterlife

BY

VIVIAN WEI

According to Chinese cultural principles, the practice of sharing an enjoyable, harmonious meal during the wake of a funeral helps to reinforce the family's connection with the deceased, ensuring that the spirit leaves the body both happy and sated. Providing a proper selection of food allows the departing spirit to have a safe journey to the heavens and provide protection to their family on earth.

Wagga

As I wove through the strands of waist-high panicum weed, the sun began to settle behind the golden hills of endless patchwork farmland. The grass tickled my exposed knees and poked at my ankles. A distant '*moo*' swept past me on the breeze but was soon drowned out by the chatter of cicadas and grasshoppers, their constant noise filling the empty, open field. I bounced up a little as my *Ong* helped to readjust my bag, relieving me of the pocket of heat that had started to settle across my lower back. My feet followed the worn trail of dirt as the grass became shorter and shorter, leading us to a small creek that meandered through low-hanging branches. I slumped against a flaking tree trunk as my *Ong* pulled two nashi pears from his backpack and handed one to me.

~

The air was thick and oily, heavy with the pungent scent of sesame and garlic. The old ventilation system whirred and clunked in the background before coming to a sudden stop. My father walked over and smacked the grimy plastic housing of the fan with the wooden handle of his cleaver. The fan groaned in protest and went back to work.

I ducked through my father's legs to reach my *Ong's*, hidden under his navy-blue-striped, batter-smeared apron. His legs were strong and sturdy like tree trunks. He carried me back and forth to the refrigerator as I clung to him like an infant monkey.

At the river near the tree trunk, I crouched beside my *Ong* and splayed my fingers in the water, watching them sweep back and forth through the ripples. It was cool and clear, flowing gently, hypnotically. We sat in silence, sharing each other's company as we crunched into the pears and slurped to catch the sweet juice dribbling out of the corners of our mouths.

Ong had often taken me to this place. He liked to describe how the tiny lights in the sky could only be seen here, far away from the city, after the sun had gone to bed. Each time, he would tell me that these tiny lights belonged to many different families, all with their own worries, joys and places in society. I would hold his hand as we sat together, kneading it gently, rubbing at the lumps and spots on his skin in the hope of removing them and somehow restoring his youth.

~

My father called out, '*Lǎobǎn!*'

I stopped tracing patterns in the sink with my fingers amongst the soaking bok choy leaves. '*Lǎobǎn*' was a respectful term, literally translating to 'old boss'. Father walked up next to me and snatched at the bok choy, shaking the leaves to rid them of excess water. There was a crisp crunch as his knife sliced through the layers of leaves, followed by a soft scrape as the mountainous green pile was pushed into a clear plastic container. Father bent over and slid the case into the silver fridge beside the sink, shutting the door with a thud. Preparation for the Tuesday dinner rush was well underway in The Golden Duck Restaurant in downtown Wagga.

I was fourteen when I heard about the passing of *Ong*. I felt cold from the announcement of his death, as though a piece of my own body had been suddenly ripped away; not a limb or anything physical, but something much deeper and much more important than that. I sat heavily, wondering if I had kneaded his once-strong hands enough, and whether I could've kneaded him back to good health when I saw him last if I'd tried a little harder.

China

The plane tyres touched down on the tarmac of Zhōngguó, the passengers greeted by familiar surroundings. Gone now were the social graces that had been adopted for life in Australia: the passengers shoved each other to retrieve their stowed bags and pushed their way through to the exit.

The pungent smell was distinct… ancient… damp. Sewage air mingled with lingering cigarette smoke, exhaled only from the lips of wealthy men. A raspy '*ach*' followed promptly by the '*tooey*' of a spit globule flying from the janitor's mouth jolted me with disgust. It landed on the tiles beside my feet, the janitor then proceeding to casually smear the spit across the ground with his mop. I was back in the familiar city that was my family's hometown: Fuzhou, Fujian province of the great almighty motherland of China.

It was dark and cold when we made it out of the airport. Wisps of snow whipped through the grey air. Driving back to my grandmother's place in our second uncle's car, I stared out the window as high-rise buildings filled the sky and then disappeared again. Neon Chinese symbols flashed along streets packed with food stalls. Bright yellow streetlights beamed down on rows of glistening roast duck, strung up along streets bursting with people.

My grandma was a loving woman who we called *ma-ma*, pronounced with a higher inflection than the pronunciation of 'mother' in Chinese. I flicked on the lights as I entered her house and halted when I first caught a glimpse of the dark room. *Ong*'s light-blue striped pyjamas lay neatly folded on the end of his bed, and his khaki-coloured coat hung crinkled on the doorknob. Hot tears pricked at my eyes and I gave them an aggressive wipe.

During dinner, I sat to face the front door. When I was a child, *Ong* would usually return home, late from fishing, halfway through our feast. This time, we finished dinner without that familiar click in the keyhole, so I brushed my teeth staring at his frayed toothbrush and put myself to bed in the room next to his. I waited, longing to hear the quiet *knock-knock* on the wall that *Ong* usually did to say goodnight. Instead, I fell asleep to soft sounds of crickets singing their lullabies in the distance.

The Duck

The spirit must cross three rivers on its way to the heavens—the Gold River, the Silver River and the Yin/Yang River. The duck symbolises protection for the spirit as it makes its journey across the water.

There have been two dishes of duck I've eaten throughout my childhood: home-cooked and restaurant-style.

The restaurant-style duck was lathered in oil, its outer skin crispy and glistening a cherry red. It was rolled out by the waiter on a huge plate and sliced into pieces at the table. We wrapped the duck in soft, chewy pancakes, along with sticks of cucumber and some roughly-chopped spring onions. Biting into the pancake, your tongue was coated with the salty hoisin sauce as your teeth sank into the succulent meat; if you didn't slurp quickly enough, you'd find yourself with juices trailing down your arm. We would all smile, wiping our oily fingers on our napkins before handing around another pancake.

The home-cooked duck wasn't fancy, nor was it glistening

in oil. It was just a simple dish, but one on which *Ong* had prided himself. The duck was braised in a simple base of star anise, garlic, cloves, wine and soy sauce—a recipe that had been added to over generations. I don't know exactly what our family recipe was, but it brought us together at dinner, where we wrapped ourselves around the table with bowls of steaming rice. This dish was one that you shared memories with at the table.

We listened to my *ma-ma*'s stories about her day at the street market or grocery store; about rising meat prices, or ridiculously cheap longans (which explained the red bags bursting with the fruit at the rosewood table in the living room), or about an incident with another grandmother at the store who shoved rudely past at the seafood stalls.

The duck would allow my *Ong* to swim through to the heavens, but it also allowed our family to swim through memories when we shared the dish at his funeral.

Sydney

The decision to move from Anglo-centric Wagga Wagga to the cultural melting pot that was Sydney—for my education—was made just days prior to the beginning of a school term.

My Sydney school was multicultural and prided itself on its diversity. I'd never known a race other than 'Australian' or 'Chinese', and being one of only two Chinese kids in primary school, it was a real culture shock when I realised I lacked knowledge of not only my own race, but of my new classmates'.

On my first day at my new school, I was approached by a short, stocky Asian boy who began speaking to me in a rapid-fire and aggressive tone. I shook my head and threw up my hands. In perfect English he replied, 'Oh sorry, I thought you were Korean.'

In Sydney, I learned that culture dictated style. For the Chinese, the price often seemed more important than style. It didn't matter if the ensemble was ugly, as long as it was expensive. It was different, though, for the Koreans; they seemed to have a more adventurous eye for fashion.Back in Wagga, I was just the 'the Asian one' and we all paired board shorts with muscle tees or crop tops purchased from Cotton On, on Baylis Street.

When we lived in Wagga, we visited China once a year. But after we moved to Sydney, that was no longer the case. It was partially due to the high cost of living but, mostly, it was because we were immersed in the greater Chinese culture that Sydney had to offer. Chinatown was less than half an hour's train ride away, and a walk down Dixon Street offered an exclusive tour through the culinary history and geography of a vast array of Chinese towns and provinces. All the restaurants offered standard Chinese fare, but each would proudly offer specialties found only in their home region.

The area in Sydney where my family chose to settle had a thriving Asian culture, with its own Asian shopping centre—dirty in comparison to the western shopping centre down the road, spotless in comparison to the ones in China.

In Wagga, nobody ever commented on how I looked different, but I often felt that it was implied. Here, I finally felt comfortable in my own skin. I knew my parents felt the same way, as they could easily speak to the residents in our neighbourhood in a different language without receiving odd looks. There was no longer a reason or a yearning to return home to China.

At first, I found myself bewildered by the various cultures that existed side by side in Sydney. Like in any modern, sprawling metropolis, different cultures and ethnicities 'belonged' in certain suburbs. Out in the west, the Vietnamese quarter was in Cabramatta, while the Middle Eastern sector was Granville and its outlying suburbs. Harris Park through to Wentworthville was the Indian quarter. Eastwood was split into two sections by a line that ran right through the train station, separating the Chinese and the Koreans. The richer Anglos could be found along the Northern Beaches, and the poorer out in Penrith. It was fascinating.

In Sydney, you could experience another country on the tip of your tongue. If you knew where to look, you would have no problem finding a cosy restaurant tucked away in a secret alleyway in the city, the scents of garlic and turmeric hanging in the air. My teeth have pulled at authentic Korean seared meats, my tastebuds have been hit by the saltiness of briny Japanese noodle broths, and I've had my tongue numbed by aromatic, vibrant Indian curries.

In Sydney, the world was on your plate.

~

China

I turned my mind to the vibrant night markets that sold cheap notebooks and cute junk, purchased impulsively, becoming useless once brought home.

The food was abundant, especially the fruit—dramatically cheaper and richer in taste. I sucked on mangosteen that coated my tongue in a sickly-sweet juice, munched into dragon fruit with seeds that stayed stuck between my teeth, and ate through endless bags of longan, juices dribbling down my chin.

The streets were dirty, but I felt comfortable. A gentle shoulder bump with a stranger wouldn't cause a potential issue here, as it could in Sydney.

Side streets were laden with food stores, selling freshly-fried Chinese pancakes, dripping in oil. Meat stores were piled high with chicken feet and fatty pig intestines, and customers filled small plastic bags with the meat to snack on, on their way home.

No government officials checked health or safety regulations. Unless you were a foreigner, nobody minded where the food or chef certificates were kept, or, for that matter, if they even existed. Reputation counted for more.

During a traditional Chinese funeral, the deceased is offered various plates of food, each dish having great significance in contributing to the safe journey of a spirit into the heavens.

~

My *Ong* was offered the traditional dishes of meat, vegetables and rice. This happened for many days, and once each day ended, the mourners would then eat the offerings. Years ago, when my great-grandfather or great-great-grandfather passed, there would have only been a limited amount of food due to the lack of wealth, so only certain dishes were chosen as offerings. The community already struggled to keep themselves fed, but the Chinese are proud, so to be too poor to send someone to the heavens was unspoken of.

Tradition was tradition, and nobody wanted to be haunted by an angry spirit.

Now, there was wealth, and we feasted upon the juices of the symbolic animal we offered that day, our teeth sinking into its flesh without any sense of gratitude or remorse. To me, these offerings that were supposed to be full of reflection and respect felt hollow because we could go to any Chinese restaurant—in China or Australia—and gorge on the same meals.

At night, a spiral-shaped incense stayed lit to guide my *Ong* through his journey to the heavens. The cold, concrete walls of the living room were unevenly paved, as my father had constructed them with child-sized hands when he was younger. In this room, my uncle slept by the coffin and incense, waking every other hour to offer more rice to my grandfather's spirit, or to relight the incense stick. Every night, I watched the match head crackle against the flint of the box and burst into a small bright flame before kissing the spiral of delicate bamboo, the faint fragrance of jasmine filling the room. Once the sun woke in the morning, my *Ong* would be able to find his way during the day, though we offered more food to protect him during this journey.

When *Ong*'s ashes were sprinkled into his concrete grave, we placed plates of fruit around the front of it, along with some *yu wan*. His portrait was leaned against the headstone carefully, to identify his resting place from the other thousand graves that were clustered along the mountain top. My grandfather's favourite bread biscuits were stacked on a plate for him to eat, and to share around with his new friends who were travelling on the same journey to heaven. There was no outpouring of grief, no wailing or gnashing of teeth. Our grief was tightly funnelled into tradition and routine. Tears were crushed in favour of cultural mores.

Yu wan—which translates to 'fish ball'—originated from Fuzhou, 'back home'. One of my favourite childhood dishes, it was the comfort food of choice during winters. Three or four of these fish balls floated in a hot, clear, noodle-filled soup. *Ong* used to sit me on the kitchen counter as he prepared the *yu wan*. He had an economy of movement that I have never seen since; each step was performed with precision in a flawless ballet of muscle memory and years of discipline.

Ong loved this dish, and so I prepared it to be offered at his funeral. A large proportion of the offerings were made to my grandfather's liking, so he could embark on his journey happily.

~

The Cock

The cock holds a rich place in ancient Chinese history, in both divination and cockfighting. Embracing the symbol of the sun and the yang element, it possesses the qualities of light, warmth and strength. When the deceased's body is moved to the burial site, a white-feathered cock may be placed on the coffin to banish evil spirits, allowing the soul to remain safely with the body.

Along with the *yu wan* sat a plate of a cold, shiny and yellowing sliced chicken. This was made by my *ma-ma*. I watched her falter as she set the plate down. She looked at *Ong*'s photo for a long time then turned and shuffled slowly out of the room.

Returning to mainland China for my grandfather's funeral meant that the Canadian branch of our family would also be there. Most of our family had settled in Canada, where the sun was mild in summer, hitting tops of 25 degrees on a sweltering day, and snow falling heavily in the -20-degree winters. But my family had settled where there were beautiful beaches and summers that soared into the 40s, and we considered a mild 17 degrees too cold to handle.

My Canadian cousins were brought up speaking a broken 'Chinglish' of English and Mandarin. My parents brought us up speaking our regional dialect, Fuzhounese, with a smattering of Mandarin and Cantonese. But when the Canadians came, it was only English. In China, it was thought of as 'superior' to speak this way, weaving through night markets in Fuzhou chatting in English. At the park, the other Chinese kids would stare in awe and ask us where we were from and how we learned to speak a different language. '*Zài lái, Zài lái,*' or, 'Again, again,' was always shouted. 'Teach us how to speak English!' they'd say as they giggled self-consciously at their awkward pronunciations.

My dad joked around with the locals when they asked how we spoke such fluent English, telling everyone that his kids studied at international schools. He curated a story about how they taught us to speak English fluently and taught us to love hobbies like chess, violin and basketball. In a way, it was his means of telling us that he loved us and he was proud of our achievements and how we developed as a family in Australia.

Yet this time, there was no sense of superiority, because I had lost my ability to communicate even the simplest words of the universal Chinese language and only a few knew how to speak Fuzhounese. I didn't really have anybody to share or practise the dialect with in Australia, so I stuck to English.

We stayed in China for two weeks for the mourning, celebration and funeral. Typically, the funeral offerings would continue for a cycle of forty-nine days. It was a 'seven by seven' tradition. Seven by seven weeks meant that on the seventh day of each week, another offering of food would be made. A spiral of incense was lit every day to provide energy for *Ong* to continue on his journey. On the forty-ninth day, his final offering would be given, signalling that he had reached the heavens. After each offering, we would devour pig, duck or chicken, slowly forgetting about the prayers we shared for the elderly and deceased.

Buddha's Delight (Luóhàn zhāi)

This vegetarian dish uses eighteen ingredients of particular cultural significance to represent the eighteen Buddhas. The family of the deceased may choose to abstain from eating meat during the mourning period to cleanse the body and remain pure in the eyes of the gods. The presentation of this dish also allows the deceased's spirit to be purified.

We arrived at Pu Tuo Shan for the last leg of our journey. Pu Tuo Shan is a mountain renowned for Chinese Buddhism, surrounded by traditionally-built temples and plastic-wrapped shrines. The mountain wavered high above the ground, its rugged terrain fading from a lush green to a dull ochre yellow. The architecture of the temples adhered to the structural principles of ancient Chinese Tang Dynasty design, with high, multi-tiered terracotta roofs. It was a four-hour train ride and an hour bus journey followed by thirty minutes on a cramped, rocky boat.

Because of the surrounding religious customs, it was a requirement to remain vegetarian or vegan throughout one's stay at the mountain. Breakfast, lunch and dinner were all provided, but were inevitably the same.

Breakfast was bowls of watered-down congee (to save the restaurant money). Lunch was savoury boiled potatoes, sweet chilli tofu and a crunchy kelp stir-fry dish, each presented with a communal bowl of steamed rice. Dinner was the same. But the mountain was cold and rainy, and we were soaked and hungry, so nobody complained much. The one thing people picked on, though, was the soup. Every meal was served with the same seaweed 'soup'. Hot water, dried seaweed and a drizzle of sesame oil. 'We paid to be served hot water and a sprinkling of seaweed here!' came from a lot of tables.

Each day, we made our way up a different mountain to bow to the shrines and offer incense and, if we wished, money. People would place large sums into the boxes in front of each statue of a god to prove their devotion and to ask for the spirits to watch over them and bless them with a life of prosperity. But when these same people got back on their tour bus at the end of the visit on each mountain, they discreetly peeled open vacuum-sealed packets of preserved chicken feet and sucked on them behind their seats.

On the train ride back, I was able to catch a glimpse of Chinese countryside before we disappeared into the pitch-black tunnels. There were villages scattered across the terrain, some made up of just four or five concrete buildings, with expensive black cars coming and going constantly. Other villages were filled with endless rows of green and yellow fields, where a person could be spotted bent over, hacking away tirelessly at the crops.

There was an old man who reminded me of my *Ong* standing in the middle of the green fields. The sun was setting, turning the sky a hazy orange as he strolled slowly, hands behind his back, the way all the elderly walk in China. I wondered how long it must have taken him to reach the middle of the vast, open field and if he would make it back before dark as he continued to stroll farther away from the residential buildings. He seemed at peace, enjoying the vegetation, the greenery, the sunset. He must have been able to reflect a lot on his life with this freedom, these endless views that gave enough space for his thoughts to wander far.

My *ma-ma* was a short woman with grey hair and traditional Chinese composure. She wore a thick Chinese silk blouse, decorated with flowers. Her spine was arched with age, and she wobbled a little when she walked, struggling to keep balanced. Her feet were tiny and so was she, but she had a loud voice that bossed my *Ong* around. 'Don't eat that! It's cold! Do you want to get sick? Have you had your medicine today?'

But when there was nobody to boss about anymore, she called out to him in her sleep and cried for him at the funeral. Her tiny frame seemed to shrink even smaller as we marched his coffin down the street during the ceremony, family members on either side of her to help her walk. When his body was taken to be turned into ashes, she clutched his photo to her chest. She reached out a shaking hand for someone, anyone, to hold and comfort her.

In that moment, I broke. The other relatives bowed their heads with sympathy as I ran over to my *ma-ma* to clutch her arm while she cried through memories of the man she had shared sixty years of her life with. The loss had broken her, but she was strong and we all knew she could clamber out of her mourning. She would bring her loud voice back to her children and offer home-cooked food around her table once more.

The *Buddha's Delight* was placed in a shallow dish and shared around the table. Chopsticks clipped at the plate of food, noodles dangling and bouncing off the two sticks, smothered in the thick brown sauce. With the close air of *Ong*'s funeral still present in the room, there was no talking, just the sounds of slurping as we each remembered his impact on our lives.

This dish was my favourite, the noodles soft but not overcooked and the braised tofu firm enough to give a bite on the outer skin but with a mouthful of silky softness inside. But a lump in my throat made it hard for me to swallow my food. I didn't enjoy this meal, and neither did any of us at the table.

Sydney

I bite into a bowl of *yu wan* and *bian rou* in our small but busy restaurant, tucked away in a Sydney alley. The fish balls are bouncy, and the *bian rou* casing has the perfect bite. Hot, salty soup floods my mouth and the comfort of familiarity washes over me. My father comes out of the kitchen, wiping his hands on his apron.

'Did you sort out the ABN?'

'Yes, Dad.'

'Good. We don't want those bastards on our back.'

He takes a fresh spoon and dips it into my broth, slurping loudly.

'*Ach…* too much MSG.'

As he walks back to the kitchen, I head to the door and flip the 'Closed' sign to 'Open'. I look down the long line of customers.

'We're only having two sittings today,' I announce, looking over at the picture of *Ong* on the wall.

'What's the special?'

'*Yu wan.*'

Reference:

Tang-Duffy, fortuneandflavours.com, 'Food and Chinese Funeral Practices', 2007.

Variation

BY
TOBIAS MADDEN

Every nerve in my body is tingling, ready to fire. I take in a lungful of musty air and twist my neck to one side until the joints pop.

'The next competitor is number thirty-two, Andrew Raymond,' a woman announces over the foldback speakers.

I take an assured step into the wings, draw my body up into my starting position and wait, poised for my entrance. And right at that moment, as my song begins to play, a voice starts echoing in my mind. I shake my head to dislodge his words before they have a chance to affect me, and shift my attention to my breathing.

I will not let him ruin this for me.

This is it.

This is my moment.

I count myself in—a 5, 6, 7, 8—and in an explosion of power and grace, I leap from the shadows into the blinding white lights of the stage.

Everyone thinks guys who do ballet are gay. And don't get me wrong, I'm sure most of them are. But not all of them. Not Stiefel. Not Baryshnikov.

Not me.

I'm from the kind of country town in Victoria that's only just big enough to warrant having its own Coles, but has six pubs within walking distance of each other, and four football teams.

Dad taught me to play football the minute I could walk. He loves footy. Possibly more than he loves Mum and me. Luckily, for all concerned, we love footy too.

But the thing is, I was never really any good at football. I had the right body type, and I could sprint the length of the field faster than all the other boys, but I was very lacking in the hand-eye coordination department. Plus, I couldn't kick for shit.

I kept playing for years—for Dad's sake—but I knew, deep down, that I was just wasting my time. And I've always believed that if you can't be the absolute best at something, then why bother? Why live a mediocre life doing one thing when you can be bloody brilliant doing something else?

And the thing is, I'm *really* good at ballet.

I didn't even know boys could *do* ballet until I was thirteen—well into my unexceptional football career. I remember sitting on the couch one Sunday afternoon with a packet of BBQ Shapes, flicking through boring infomercial after boring infomercial, when I stumbled upon this ancient recording of a ballet called *The Nutcracker*.

There was a man on stage, all by himself. He looked like a footy player—strong, masculine, athletic—only he was dressed like a toy soldier. And he was *dancing*.

I don't know what it was about watching this toy soldier dance, but it sparked something inside me. I stood up on the couch and watched, enrapt, as he leapt—no, *flew*—around the stage in this big, sweeping circle. It was like he could defy the laws of physics at will.

And then, before I knew it, it was over. The crowd erupted into applause, and I just stood there, frozen, my feet glued to the couch cushion, my eyes glued to the TV screen.

In that moment, all I could think about was my Year 7 English teacher. She always used to tell us we needed to find our true 'calling' in life. She'd then make the same awkward joke about how her calling was definitely *not* teaching Shakespeare to a bunch of smelly Year 7s, but here she was! The point is, standing there on the couch watching that toy soldier bow, I finally understood what she meant.

I took a deep breath and called out to Mum in the kitchen: 'Mum, am I allowed to be a ballerina?'

Of course, Mum thought it was a bit—as she put it at the time—'funny' for a thirteen-year-old boy to want to dress up in tights and prance around with a bunch of girls in tutus. And, trust me, in my town, it was considered funny. Where I came from, no one had even seen the film *Billy Elliot*, let alone an actual ballet. But I didn't care. Somehow, I just *knew* I was going to be brilliant at ballet.

As if it were meant to be—which, I dunno, I guess you could say it was—there was a dance studio literally around the corner from our house, perched on top of Johnson's Hardware. I'd walked past it every day on the way to school, but never actually noticed it—which was saying something, because the words 'The Polly Higgins School of Ballet' were plastered on the front of the building in fluoro pink letters.

A big part of me thought the idea of rocking up to Miss Polly's little studio every Wednesday and Friday night was a reputation-ruining, soul-destroyingly bad idea, but, despite the threat of being endlessly taunted for the rest of my teenage life, ballet was calling. So I enrolled for Term 2.

And then, after making me promise I wouldn't tell Dad anything about it until she worked out how to 'soften the blow', Mum took me shopping for dance clothes. Well, that little excursion turned out to be a *mortifying* ordeal, didn't it? Having to discuss the *padded G-string* I needed to wear under my tights—and the safe way to *position myself* inside it—in front of my mother was enough to make me want to be swallowed up by the earth on the spot.

But still, ballet was calling. Louder and louder.

The lights are so bright I can't see the audience. Which means I can't be distracted by Mum's nervous grin, or be thrown off by the other parents' cocky expressions, each and every one of them secretly praying I'll screw up.

It's like no one is there, like I'm totally alone.

Just me and the music.

I chaîné, I grand jeté, I pirouette, I sissonne—perfectly.

It's like coming first in a hundred-metre sprint. Like holding up the premiership cup. That sense of fulfilment? That exhilaration, that ecstasy? That's what I feel for every count of choreography I nail. And the more steps I execute in perfect succession, the more that feeling multiplies, until nothing else could ever possibly come close to feeling that good.

Frankly, I don't know why teenagers waste their time on drugs and sex and alcohol when they could be dancing instead.

When I walked into my very first ballet class, the only thought in my head was, 'Don't get hard.'

It was the first time I'd worn my tights in public, and I was a typically hormonal teen, about to walk into a studio full of pretty girls in leotards. I knew how to hide a boner at school— carrying big textbooks always worked a treat—but in a pair of tights? Impossible. And if the unthinkable happened at Miss Polly's studio, there was no way in holy *hell* I could ever show my face there again. Thankfully, it turned out that the mere thought of pitching a tent in my tights during class was stressful enough to stop it from actually happening.

My second thought—once I'd calmed myself down—was, 'This is where I belong.'

The studio was small, with wooden floorboards, two long ballet barres screwed to opposite walls, and a whole wall of mirrors. The afternoon sun beamed through the windows and glanced off the mirrors, casting a glow over this one particular spot at the barre, which was where I always stood.

It felt more like home than my house ever did.

It turned out Polly Higgins had died about forty years ago and the ballet school was now run by her granddaughter, Miss Izzy, who was thirty-something and totally hot. Like most ballerinas, she was super thin, but really strong. 'Lithe' was the word my mum had used to describe her, and she'd said it with so much envy that it almost sounded like an insult. But despite whatever Mum *really* wanted to call her, I had a major crush on Miss Izzy. And it wasn't as if Miss Izzy had a crush on *me*—she had a husband and kids, and I was a pimply thirteen-year-old boy, for God's sake—but I knew she had a soft spot for me.

She said something to me once, about six months into my training, and I'll never forget it: 'I'll only get to work with a handful of students like you in my life, Andrew.' And she'd danced with the Royal Ballet in London—until she screwed her knee and had to come home—so I knew she knew her shit. But no one had ever implied that I was special before. Not at school, not at footy, not even at home. So, at first, I didn't know whether to take her seriously or not. But then I started to see it too. I was different from the girls I danced with. Some of them had nice technique, and were lucky enough to be born with the right body type—the 'facility' as Miss Izzy called it—but none of them picked things up as quickly as I did. None of them shared my passion, my ambition.

Miss Izzy was right: I *was* special.

She also told me it was okay to be confident about my skills, but that there was a fine line between confidence and arrogance. She said if I wanted to become a self-obsessed bastard who'd die cold and alone in his Covent Garden flat surrounded by nothing but awards, I could go ahead and be arrogant. If not, I should stick with confident. She had a special way with pep talks, Miss Izzy.

By the time I was fifteen, I'd won all the major country-Victorian eisteddfods, and Miss Izzy said I was ready to compete in the Open Classical Championship at the Ballarat Eisteddfod: the Holy Grail of Victorian ballet comps. She said that if I won that, I could start seriously thinking about auditioning for the Australian Ballet School. Not that winning the Championship guaranteed a dancer a place at ABS, but the list of past winners pretty much *all* went on to study there. The Championship was a stepping stone—and a vital one at that.

My heart beats in time with the music. I can feel the rhythm of it in my bones, guiding my every movement. I feel electric, cutting across the stage like a spark of pure energy. My legs are coils of steel, my arms flowing silk. Sweat drips down my forehead under the heat of the lights, but nothing can bother me now.

I'm in the zone.

These three minutes on stage right now, this is where I find my joy. This is where I feel worthy, where I'm truly myself. No matter what some dickhead just said to me. No matter—

Focus, Andy. Just listen to the music.

This is your moment.

Do not waste it.

Picture me, sitting my dad down in the lounge room and telling him I wanted to be a *professional* ballet dancer. That I wanted to audition for a full-time ballet school in Melbourne at the end of the year. His response? He said I'd made a big enough fool out of myself as it was, and that prancing around like a poof as a hobby was one thing, but being a professional prancing poof was another.

And then came the silent treatment.

Mum said to give him some time, that he just needed to 'deal with it'.

Deal with *what*? The fact that I was exceptionally talented? That I was good enough to go to the Australian Ballet School someday? If Dad had listened to a single word I'd said at the dinner table over the past two years he would have known how rare that was, how few people ever got the chance to dance professionally.

'Deal with it.' I mean, come *on*.

Thankfully, I had the Open Classical Championship to focus on. If I won that, it would prove to Dad that I was legit, that I wasn't just prancing around for shits and giggles, that I *deserved* to go to ABS.

So I really needed to win.

And then, literally the next afternoon, I walked into the studio and there was this stranger standing at the ballet barre. A *male* stranger. Tall. Blond. Wearing a purple unitard and white ballet shoes, with white socks pulled halfway up to his knees. He had *perfect* feet and *perfect* calves and his body was the *perfect* mix of slender and muscular coveted by every male dancer in the universe.

My stomach dropped, and my chest fluttered with a strange, unfamiliar mix of excitement and terror.

Miss Izzy flounced into the studio, clearly on cloud bloody nine, and said, 'Andrew, I'd like you to meet Kyle Shepherd, our new student. He'll be in Advanced One with you.'

Kyle Shepherd turned from the barre, smiling with a set of pristine white teeth that matched his pristine white socks.

'Hi,' he said.

And everything I'd worked so hard for crumbled to pieces around me.

It turned out Kyle had just moved up from Melbourne. Something to do with his parents wanting their kids to grow up with 'country values', or something ridiculous like that. Kyle was the same age as me, which meant not only did I have to put up with him at ballet, I had to put up with him at school as well. And let me tell you, I'd never disliked anyone more than Kyle Shepherd.

He was the first openly gay student my school had ever had, which, you know, is fine. Whatever. Be gay. It's 2019, be whatever the hell you want. But he acted as if 'gay' was his only personality trait. Like, if he were a cartoon, he'd have been drawn exclusively with glitter pens. And he'd be holding a rainbow flag. Eating fairy floss. Riding a unicorn.

For weeks and weeks I told myself not to be a dickhead about it and to just accept Kyle for who he was, because he actually seemed like a really nice guy. But, for some reason, the nicer he was to me, the more I couldn't stand him. Wherever he went, he was always smiling and laughing and dancing. Always bloody dancing. We'd be in Maths and I could see him practising *entrechat quatres* under the table. We'd go to Red Rooster with the girls after ballet and he'd be literally *jeté*-ing down the aisle between the tables. It was beyond infuriating.

All the girls at school loved him, of course, but the guys thought he was a total joke—and they weren't afraid to show it. I think what bothered me the most about Kyle was that he literally didn't care what anyone thought about him. Schoolyard taunts were nothing but water off a bright pink duck's back for Kyle. Any other boy at our school would have dissolved into a pool of sweat and grease and hair product if they were teased as much as Kyle was, but he would always just laugh, toss some imaginary hair over his shoulder and walk away.

And no matter how hard I tried to avoid him, we always crossed paths in the corridors. He'd give me a playful little wave and smile his perfect little smile, and I'd be overcome by a sudden, inexplicable urge to trip him over.

Of course, as soon as the other boys noticed these small but frequent interactions, there was a sudden resurgence in the number of insults being slung my way.

'Where's your boyfriend today, Dandy *Gay*mond?' they started asking me on the bus. Every single morning, the same question. I mean, get some new material.

'He's not my boyfriend,' I'd reply.

'Do you wear a tutu when he does you from behind?' one of

them asked me one morning.

I punched him in the face.

Not my finest moment. Though Dad seemed weirdly happy about it when I brought home my detention slip. It was the first time since I'd quit footy that I'd seen him display any amount of paternal pride. I guess that's pretty messed up, but… whatever.

And to top it all off, there was the fact that Kyle was unequivocally, indisputably, really fucking good at ballet.

'Look at Kyle's *épaulement*, everyone,' Miss Izzy would say. Or, 'Watch Kyle's feet in his *cabriole*, Andy.'

His elevation was better than mine. He had better extension, better feet. He could do more *pirouettes* than I could. His package even looked bigger in his tights than mine did.

If dirty looks could kill, I would have slain Kyle Shepherd a hundred times over.

I'm dancing better than I ever have in the studio—I even add an extra pirouette *at one point without trying. Everything is easy. Everything is perfect. And then his face materialises in the glare of the lights.*

'Aren't you sick of it?' *he says.* 'Aren't you exhausted?'

I hesitate for a moment—a fraction of a second—and I'm suddenly behind the music. I am no longer focused, no longer in the zone.

'That's why you hate me so much.' *His voice is booming in my ears.* 'You're—'

I fumble a step and pause, right on centre stage. I'm completely lost. Panic floods my mind, drenching me in doubt.

What comes next? What's the next step?

The music continues to play, leaving me for dead.
Think, Andy! Come on. Think. *Get it together!*
But my mind is empty. I have no fucking clue what comes next…

'There's one more dancer, and then you'll be up, honey,' the bushy-haired stage manager said, giving me a motherly pat on the back.

I was in the green room, surrounded by girls in tutus. The Ballarat Eisteddfod was one of the biggest ballet competitions of the year for Victorian dancers. And for me, the two-hour trip to and from Ballarat every day for a week was totally worth it for the prize money and exposure. I'd competed both years since I started ballet—and won every section I entered—but I'd never competed in the Open Classical Championship. And I'd never competed against Kyle Shepherd.

'Thanks,' I said to the stage manager, just as Kyle burst into the green room from the stage, drenched with sweat.

'And *that*,' he said, strutting through the sea of tulle, 'is how you nail a variation.'

A girl in an outrageously pink tutu galloped over to him in a fit of squeals, prompting Kyle to squeal too. I rolled my eyes and turned to face the wall, pressing against it to stretch out my calves.

From the moment we'd walked through the stage door that morning, I'd wanted to knock Kyle out. If I thought I'd seen him at his most flamboyant, I'd never seen him at a ballet comp.

'How you feeling?' someone asked from behind me, panting.

'Fine,' I said, refusing to turn around. I knew it was Kyle, and I couldn't bear to look at his smug face.

'The stage is a bit slippery in a couple of spots down the front, you might want to—'

'Got it,' I said to the wall, gritting my teeth.

'Andy, are you all right?'

'I'm fine.'

'Then, why won't you look at me?'

I whipped around to face him. 'Look, do you mind? I'm trying to warm up, okay?'

'*Okay*,' he said, frowning. 'Well…' And then he leaned in, hugged me around the shoulders and kissed me on the cheek.

'What the f—' I pushed him away.

'Whoa, Andy,' he replied, grinning awkwardly. 'I was just going to say good luck.'

'Well, just don't, all right?' I said, glancing around to see if anyone had noticed him hugging me.

'Are you sure you're okay?' he said, his eyes narrowed.

'I'm *fine*.' But I couldn't look him in the eye. 'And I don't need you to wish me luck.'

'It's okay to be nervous,' Kyle said. 'It's a big competition.'

'I'm not nervous.'

'Then why are you being so weird? Is there something you want to talk about?'

He really didn't know when to shut up. This time, I ignored him. I walked over to the costume rack and grabbed my jacket.

'Look,' he said, tailing me, 'it's not good to dance if you've got something on your mind.'

I slipped the brocaded jacket on over my unitard and zipped it up at the front.

'Andy?'

'What?' I snapped, turning to face him. 'What do you want?'

'I want to help.'

'We're not *friends*, Kyle,' I said, drenching my voice in as much contempt as I could manage. 'And I don't need your help.'

Kyle folded his arms across his chest. 'Why do you have to be like this? What the hell did I ever do to you?'

'Give it a rest.'

'No,' he said. 'Ever since I moved here you've been a total asshole to me, no matter how hard I tried to be nice to you.' He swept his wet fringe back from his face. 'What did I ever do to you? Is it because I'm a better dancer than you? Is that it?'

I scoffed. 'Fuck off, Kyle, don't try and throw me off my game.'

'If that's all it is, then that is so incredibly childish. I've worked so hard to get where I am today, and—'

'It's not that,' I snapped back at him in a harsh whisper. 'It's because you came in here today, mincing around like you own the joint, and then you go and *kiss* me in front of everyone.'

Kyle looked baffled. 'What does *that* have to do with anything?'

'They're all gonna think I'm gay, that's what.'

He snorted. 'Wow, Andy. I knew you were an asshole, but I didn't think you were a *homophobic* asshole.'

'I'm not—' I reduced my voice to a whisper '—homophobic, and can you just keep your bloody voice down? I'm not. I just don't want everyone to think I'm—'

'Gay? Because you hugged another boy?' Kyle groaned. 'Jesus Christ. I fucking hate country people. You're all the same.'

'I'm entitled to my opinion.' Sometimes I sounded so much like my dad.

'No,' he said flatly, 'you're not. Not on *my* life and how I want to live it.' He turned away and then whipped back around towards me, his cheeks flushed with anger. 'You know what? I've wanted to say this for a really long time, but I always bit my tongue because I didn't want to hurt your feelings. But do you know what I think, Andy? I think *you're* gay. And that's why you hate me so much. Because I represent everything you hate about yourself.'

'Fuck you, Kyle.'

'*Ugh*, you're always acting so damn macho,' he said, shaking his head. 'Aren't you sick of it? Aren't you exhausted?'

'I'm not *acting* anything.'

'Whatever,' he replied. 'Just do me a favour and stop taking your shit out on me. I can't help it that I'm out and proud and fucking fabulous, and you're just another sad-old, country-boy closet case.'

And with that, Kyle turned on his heel and bounded off down the stairs to the dressing rooms.

I just stood there, gaping after him, until someone tapped me on the shoulder.

'Andrew?' the stage manager said, her clipboard poised at the ready. 'You're up, honey.'

I stand there for an eternity, praying that on the outside I still look calm, poised, strong. Because on the inside, I am dying.

I manage to fudge my way through a set of basic chassé *turns to give my brain time to shake free of the panic. The turns aren't impressive, but they're better than just standing there on the spot like a complete fuckwit. As I turn, I hear the violins on my track move through a dramatic crescendo and, as if a fuse has suddenly been switched back on in my brain, I remember which part of the choreography I'm up to.*

I breathe in the sweet, intoxicating scent of relief. My brain-freeze will have cost me a bunch of points, but I can still do this, I can still win…

I nail my next set of jumps, move faultlessly through an intricate chain of footwork—my 'lightning-feet' section, as Miss Izzy calls it—and find myself centre stage again, ready for the final challenge.

I prepare for my pirouettes à la seconde, *my feet planted firmly on the stage, my eyes drilling holes into the haze of light before me. And just as I start to turn, Kyle's voice infiltrates my mind once more.*

'I'm a better dancer than you.'

Fuck off, Kyle. Not now.

'You're always acting so damn macho.'

I turn and turn and turn, willing myself to stay focused.

'You're just another sad-old, country-boy closet case.'

I'm a spinning top. Perfectly balanced.

'You're *gay*.'

In my mind, I laugh. It's completely ridiculous. Kyle Shepherd doesn't even know me. The fact that he thinks I could... that I'd ever want to... I mean, the idea of even kissing *a guy like Kyle is... it's just... it's insane, is what it is. I mean, I used to see guys naked at footy all the time and, yeah, I* looked *occasionally, but if I was gay, I would have, you know... when I looked at them, wouldn't I?*

No, I am not gay. I'm not. He's just fucking with me. There is no way in hell that I'm—

Pain suddenly shoots through my right knee and the lights scorch my eyes. A gasp rushes around the auditorium. Something hard and cold is pressing against my body, and it takes me a few seconds to realise it's the stage.

I'm on the ground.

I fell.

But how? My turns were perfect. I was perfect. I was—

Whispers hiss through the theatre like hungry snakes, ready to feast on my humiliation. My heart crumbles to dust inside my chest. The music continues to play as I push myself up and dart off the stage into the shadows.

This was my moment.

And now it's gone.

'Why the fuck did you say that to me?' I say as I slam the door to the male dressing room open.

Being the only two Under 16 male competitors, Kyle and I

have the dressing room to ourselves. He is sitting on the floor, stretching, his legs spread wide on the carpet. He's still wearing his tights, but he's replaced his bejewelled jacket with a grey t-shirt. He pulls his headphones out of his ears and looks up, scowling.

'Sorry?' he asks.

'Why did you say that to me?' I repeat, louder.

'I take it you didn't go so well?'

My laugh is almost hysterical. '"Didn't go so well"? I completely *fucked* it, Kyle.'

He stands up. 'What do you mean? What happened?'

'I fell out of my turns at the end. Because of *you*.'

His eyes widen. '*Me?*'

'No, the other dickhead in here with us,' I say. 'Yes, *you*. Because of that shit you said to me right before I went on stage.'

Kyle sidles past me and shuts the door gently. I move across to the other side of the dressing room, not wanting to be near him.

'Look, I'm—'

'You did that on purpose,' I spit. 'Didn't you? You just wanted to psych me out so you could win.'

Kyle just stands there, gaping at me.

'It's pathetic,' I continue. 'Just because you're so insecure about your own talent, you thought you'd try and get inside my head and throw me off.'

'Andy, that's not why I said it,' he replies, a smirk tugging at the corner of his mouth.

'Don't you bloody laugh at me!'

'I'm not,' he says, holding his hands up in an apology. 'I'm not laughing. I just can't believe you think I'd need to throw you off to win the Championship.'

'What?'

'I'm a better dancer than you,' he says, not unkindly, but as though it's not up for discussion. 'You know that. You're awesome, but you're… not quite there yet.'

'What the hell do you know?'

Kyle takes a step towards me and places his hands on his hips. 'Well… for one thing, I know that I got accepted into the Australian Ballet School for next year.'

It's like a punch in the gut, like a footy tackle that's come out of nowhere.

'I only found out a few days ago,' he says. 'Miss Izzy said not to tell you until after the eisteddfod. She didn't want to upset you.'

'What, like I'm some kind of fragile little tiny tot?'

Kyle chuckles.

'Stop fucking laughing at me!'

He holds a finger up to his mouth. '*Shhh*, will you? You're going to get us in trouble.'

I can't think straight. Not only did Kyle ruin my chances of winning today, now I find out he's going to ABS next year. So even if I'm lucky enough to get accepted for the year after, I'll have to deal with *him* being there.

'And, look,' Kyle begins, 'about before. I'm sorry if I upset you. It was not my intention to throw you off your game. I was just… I was angry. I'm sorry you messed up, but—'

'*You* messed me up,' I snap. 'I was *killing* it. Until…'

'Until what?' Kyle isn't laughing now. 'You realised I was right?'

I clench my jaw, my face burning. 'You were *wrong*,' I say, through gritted teeth. 'I am not… like you.'

'Then why did it affect you so much?' he asks, his voice measured and mild. 'Tell me, Andy, if you're not gay, why are you so mad at me right now?'

'I am not gay!' I storm across the dressing room and grab Kyle by the front of his t-shirt. He doesn't even flinch. As usual, nothing gets to Kyle Shepherd.

'I see the way you look at me,' he says, simply. 'At the studio, in class, when we're getting changed. You've always looked at me.'

'What?' I scrunch up my nose, disgusted by what he's implying.

'None of the other guys at school look at me. They tease me, they throw shit at me, they hide my stuff sometimes, but they never *look* at me like you do.'

'I don't look at you,' I reply, hearing the petulance in my own voice.

'Sure,' Kyle says. 'If you don't want to accept it now, that's fine. Maybe you'll come to terms with it in a few years. Or maybe you won't. Maybe you'll end up as one of those creepy old gay men who has a wife and children and a boyfriend on the si—'

I push Kyle up against the painted brick wall and he grunts in pain.

'What the—let go of me, Andrew.'

'Take it back,' I say, my face only an inch from his.

He stares back at me, his frosty blue eyes locked on mine.

'Take it *back*,' I repeat, tears starting to prick my eyes.

But Kyle doesn't reply. He just looks at me. And I look at him. At the ocean of calm in his eyes. At the symmetry of his nose. At the fullness of his lips. For a long moment, we just stand there in silence, our chests rising and falling in unison, breathing in each other's air.

And then I kiss him.

Even though I hate him. Even though he's a guy. Or, I dunno, maybe *because* I hate him, and *because* he's a guy. But, in that moment, I don't care. The only thing that matters is that our lips stay connected.

At first, Kyle is stunned by my sudden advance, his lips parted but not moving. But then he kisses me back, and something explodes inside my chest. Electricity darts from my lips to my brain to my fingertips to my crotch. The room starts spinning and my feet leave the ground and then, just as quickly as it started, it's over.

Kyle pulls away and says, 'You're kind of hurting my back.'

I realise I'm still pressing him against the wall and let go of his t-shirt.

'Sorry,' I say, looking at our feet.

'That was… unexpected,' he says eventually.

'Sorry,' I say again. I can't bear to look at him. I don't know if I'll ever be able to look at him—at *anyone*—ever again.

'No, no,' he says, 'don't be sorry. It was—'

I turn away and walk over to the costume rack, feeling sick to my stomach. 'It was stupid. I don't know what—I didn't mean—'

'Andy, I said—'

'No,' I cut in, 'please don't say anything. I don't know what I was thinking. It doesn't mean anything, I just—'

'*Andy*,' Kyle presses, from beside me now. 'I'm trying to say that I liked it.'

He takes my hand, gently, as if it's made of glass, and I look up. He smiles. And he kisses me.

This time, it's soft. Tender. He places his hand on the side of my neck and a tingle spreads through my entire body, making the air inside my lungs feel suddenly lighter.

There is a sharp knock on the door and a man barges in. I let go of Kyle's hand and turn away from the door, clearing my throat.

'Oh, sorry,' the man says. 'I…'

'It's okay, Dad,' Kyle says. 'We were just… debriefing.'

'I can see that,' Kyle's dad says, obviously not fooled, but definitely not offended. 'Your mum wanted me to come and see if you wanted to watch the last few girls dance from the front.'

'Sure, yeah,' Kyle replies. 'Andy, do you want to—'

'No, I'm fine,' I say, in a weak voice that doesn't even feel like it belongs to me. 'I'm gonna stay here.'

Kyle grabs a pair of trackies from the rack beside me and slides them on over his tights. 'You sure?'

'Yep.' I sit on the floor and grab my foam roller, unable to look directly at Kyle.

'Okay, see you after?'

'Yep, cool.' I keep my eyes on the carpet.

When Kyle walks out of the dressing room, his dad says, 'You danced really well, mate. Shame about that fall,' before following his son down the corridor.

I jump up, shut the door and press my back into it, my eyes closed. When I open them again, I catch sight of myself in the mirror. I walk over to it, lean down on the bench and gaze into my own eyes.

And I start to cry.

I have no idea how long I'm standing there, staring at my own reflection, but every time I wipe away my tears, fresh ones replace them.

I study my face in the mirror, expecting to see someone else staring back at me. A completely different boy. One who kisses other boys. But it's just me. Red-faced and tear-soaked, but still me. Nothing has changed.

But at the same time… everything is different.

Chemical Expression

BY
JES LAYTON

Then

Autumn knows the difference between what makes a person happy—a Macca's run after school, grabbing a pet and holding them tight—and what happiness actually is: chemicals.

Dopamine, oxytocin, serotonin, and endorphins.

Autumn scribbles Punnett squares on the inside of their wrist sometimes when nothing much is going on, and can tell you all about the near-deadly physics of *Super Mario Galaxy*, but they have no idea, absolutely none, of how they're supposed to go about getting some weed.

It's not something that's ever been covered in homeroom. Or something they've had to study for their SAC: *Where to get marijuana—please circle the appropriate choice.* But this isn't Saints College, this is Tech, this should be easy.

Their dad used to get stoned down the back of the Tech oval with his mate, Joel. While absolutely gone, they'd duct-taped a mate to the traffic lights out on the main street. Hid from teachers in a bush during class, high and giggly.

Their dad talks about Joel as if he's in love with him. Just a bit, or just in love with that life, the *before*.

Point is, the kids at Tech get away with not wearing their

uniforms. They don't get into the eighties with their ATARs—at least, not *yet*, Autumn tells themself—and they don't care all that much when they're chucked detention after detention for nicking off campus at lunch. Tech kids are the public-school kids. The bogans.

And Autumn's sure that someone here knows how to get weed.

Now

Chin cradled by their arms up on the desk, Autumn sits in their final period, English, and eyes the second hand lapping the clock's face. Conjugating verbs—rough on a normal day and pretty much impossible this late on a Friday arvo. The annex is stuffy and the guys in the back row are a stinking horde, having kicked off their shoes under the table. It's gross. Miss noticed it too, making a big show earlier of going around and opening up all the windows.

Autumn has homework to do, notes to take, but they scribble a Punnett square for attached earlobes—*EE, Ee, Ee, ee*—on their notebook. They're pulled out of their head by heavy footsteps outside. They sit up. The door opens.

A stocky white man with a shiny suit and a shiny head leans in. Where Autumn's dad's scalp is blotchy and yellow under most lights now, Sir's is freshly shaven. It's rare seeing their principal anywhere outside of Monday-morning assembly, let alone in their class.

His eyes survey the room and just as Autumn's about to

go back to their own inner surveying, Sir says, 'Sorry for interrupting. Autumn Nichols, can you collect your things and come with me, please.'

Though he's asking, it's not really a question.

It takes a second, but when it hits, Autumn's tongue grips the top of their mouth. They're still.

'Autumn,' Miss prompts, eyeing them through her specs. Autumn jerks. There's a feeling that sits on top of their chest, a numbness that folds down onto itself and spreads across their stomach and legs.

Heart rate, blood-pressure, epinephrine, that adrenaline high. The most basic of basic instincts: fight or flight. Controlled by norepinephrine. Autumn *knows* this. But still, *shit*.

They gather their things, scoop up their bag and feel Rhiannon's eyes on their back. She's probably already DMing them to make a run for it—both her hands are under the table.

Then

The plaster on the walls in the bathroom is an off-egg yellow, cracked and peeling. Autumn's fixated on it, or at least trying to be, but the writing on the wall in black texta is kind of distracting.

HAPPINESS IS PAIN

Okay, jeez. Autumn snaps a picture of it on their phone, uploads. Rhiannon, her skin the colour of Greek yoghurt, is perched up on the sink's edge, examining in pinches the tectonic rolls of fat around her waist.

They grab a picture of her too.

'Quit it.' Rhiannon kicks out at the air, her other leg swinging down to the floor, a load-bearing leg. 'Can we please not do the SAC post-mortem? I have bombed, Tum. *Bombed.* And I don't need any lip from you about it.'

Autumn watches Rhiannon forage for fluff in her belly button and thinks of 'navel gazing'.

Can they ask her? 'Can I ask you something?'

They hope Rhiannon won't laugh—she won't. Probably. Shit. She might vlog about it though:

What I Said When My Mate Asked Me For DrUgS: Smol Innocent Cinnamon Roll C O R R U P T E D.

Autumn's not sure what they're more afraid of: being caught; or being laughed at.

Rhiannon doesn't look up. 'Look, I studied, o'right? I swear, I went home with all my books, was the goodest of good girls. I read five whole—'

'Meant about weed.'

She looks up then. 'Weeds?'

'No, y'know, like… marijuana?' Tetrahydrocannabinol and cannabinol.

There's a full second there where neither of them says anything.

Then, Rhiannon's expression splits, lighting her up from inside. 'OM-Effen-G, Tum.' She buries her phone in the side of her bra, leaning far enough forward to tip completely off the sink. 'That's *priceless.*'

'It is?'

'*Nah*, it's like, thirty bucks or something, right? But the first pressing issue here is, why you asking me?'

'You're… worldly,' Autumn tries, ignoring the fact that they couldn't exactly ask anyone else. 'Dunno. Do you know who I *should* be asking, then?'

'A psychiatrist.'

'Be serious.'

'You know Sheridan Connelly?'

Autumn can't say they *know* Sheridan Connelly even though everyone knows Sheridan Connelly. Knows of him, really, is the better way to put it, 'cause knowing a person isn't just knowing their name.

'He's in Twelve,' Rhiannon goes on, 'wears them boots, has a fringe like this.' She cuts one finger straight across her forehead, covering her brows.

'Yeah, I seen him.'

Rhiannon shrugs. 'Yeah, well, he'd know.'

'He'd know or he'd be holding?'

'"Holding"? Effen-heck, Tum, what have you been watching?' Rhiannon hikes one knee up to her chest. As she shakes her head, the rest of her wriggles. 'Seriously, though, promise if you get anything, you'll share.'

The bell goes, Autumn heads out the bathroom door as Rhiannon jumps to her feet.

''M serious. Like, I've never tried it, right? Y'know, there's just some things you've gotta try once isn't there? Like, your dad, y'know, you said he used to—'

Autumn speed-walks past the group playing handball near the steps. They dodge the ball when it flies to them, don't stop or try to fling it back. The second bell goes, a demand now, not a warning.

Rhiannon catches up. 'You didn't even think about it, did you?' she asks.

'It?'

Her face is a *look*. 'Giving *it* a try?' She mimes turning her head to blow smoke away with two fingers pressed to her lips. Her hands flash with nails, acrylic ones she's painted with glitter. They click as she gestures and it's weirdly soothing. Autumn kind of wishes they could grow out their own stubs, but they keep eating them.

'Autumn?'

They bury the ends of their nails into their palm, the sensation barely penetrating. They think of their dad. 'It's—I'm not into that.'

They should talk to Rhiannon, they know they should talk to Rhiannon, but they won't, don't and, instead, think about whether it's possible to jump out of their life, out of their own skin.

Now

The vein in Sir's neck pulses like a blue-tongue on a rock. He asks, walking a little way ahead of Autumn, if they know why they've been called out of class.

Autumn doesn't know and says as much.

Sir's brow-ridge is huge when he looks at them over his shoulder. 'No?'

Autumn scratches at a freckle that might be dirt. 'No, sir.'

Sir hums.

It's a quiet walk down H-Wing, everyone pretty much in class. Flanked on either side by hundreds of beige lockers, Autumn drags their feet with their head down, hands curled around their shoulder straps. Fight or flight, they're faster than Sir, they could run. It might not be anything though, it might be—

Sir stops. 'Autumn, your locker, please.'

Another non-question. Autumn takes him to it.

Sir says, 'Open it, please.'

So, they do.

Then

Rhiannon messages right after class asking if Autumn wants her to go with them but, feeling a little like they're in a Marvel movie, Autumn sends back: *No. I need to do this by myself.*

However, heading towards the back of the oval, they feel as though they could've used an assembled team to get through this.

Autumn lets out a breath, their body is tight, as though they're on the edge of something—a building, a ledge... tears, maybe?

There are teachers out on duty—there are always teachers

out. Autumn's never really paid them that much attention, not during lunch and breaks. Attention is for class, for assembly, breaks are for Rhiannon and, depending on any upcoming SACs, study.

Breaks aren't for this. For *breaking* the law like this.

There's a lacka band ball fit to bursting in Autumn's chest.

There are lines their dad seems to have privately made between them and his past. He tells them that he's done drugs before, but never really gives details. He doesn't skip the edibles he ate with mates before his Year 11 formal, but doesn't ever really say what it was like. Autumn supposes he doesn't want to make drugs sound good, but all those stories are, admittedly, the exciting ones.

None of this has been exciting so far.

Autumn's nerve endings feel fried.

Rhiannon sends them a message saying Sheridan's down the back of the oval.

Of course, Autumn texts back—because where else would Sheridan be?—and gets back *Smartarse*, in response.

They stand there off the oval, looking down it, looking around. Footy players, students, trees, no teachers. Footy players, students, trees, still no teachers. Autumn's regressed to all kneecaps and tension. They smooth out their shorts, their shirt. The lacka band ball in their chest coils tight. Flexes.

They know there's a difference between being a smartarse and being intelligent and, to be honest, they're not exactly sure where Sheridan Connelly stands on that spectrum, metaphysically, that is, but they have a working theory: intelligent people do well in school and don't break the law on school property. Smartarses stand against the back fence on the oval, under the shade of some gums.

Sheridan's there, on his phone, but his chin is lifted. He's watching Autumn stomp through the weeds and gumnuts to get to him, giving the sloppy footy players a wide berth. Sheridan's about as thin as Autumn, taller, though, with long hair pulled back from his face by a hair tie, showing off a fringe you could rule lines with. Every part of his clothing some faded shade of black.

He's not a bad guy, Autumn thinks, just not the type they'd ever hang out with. Talk to. Meet eyes as they pass each other in the hallway.

But now they're gonna have a go at all three.

Sheridan taps something out on his phone. 'Hey,' he says and smiles a cortisol grin. His mouth is all braces. He's got a rubber tie on either side of his teeth, one purple, the other blue. Kind of distracting when he speaks. They stand out against all the black.

'Uhh, hey,' Autumn says.

So far. So good.

'What's up?'

'Ummm.'

Abort. ABORT.

Sheridan's phone sounds and, without looking away, his thumb moves across the screen. His hold on it is loose—there are plastic spines poking out through his fingers. His phone case looks deadly.

'Nice case.' The words come out of Autumn without them really thinking about it. They reach for their own phone as a coping mechanism. 'Love the, uh, the pseudo-hipster-post-punk-wave thing.'

Autumn's phone doesn't have a cover, just a protective screen, already shattered in one corner. They thumb at the spot where sticky tape meets glass, stare down at it.

It's in looking up that they realise Sheridan is watching them, the corners of his mouth upturned.

He's amused. Shit, but words pour from Autumn's throat, a leaky tap in the night. 'Wanna get one for, uh, my phone! Maybe… something nice, umm… y'know, dark though, stainless steel or…' Are steel phone cases even a *thing*? A thing Sheridan would be into? They have no idea. Autumn puts a hand to their collarbone, feeling skinny and cold. *Young.* 'Or something that has something on the side? I dunno, a skull or something, umm—'

'Don't cut yourself on your own edge, mate,' says Sheridan.

Autumn's mouth shuts with a painful snap. Has it been five minutes or five hours since they opened their mouth and catapulted all credibility into the sun?

Sheridan just looks at them, his smile toothy. 'Did you… want something? Or?'

'Or,' Autumn blurts.

Sheridan waits.

'Umm...' There are no alarms yet. The closest kids to them are the guys playing footy, suitably distracted. They can't see a teacher around, don't know who they should be looking out for on duty anyway. They've never had to be worried about being caught at anything before. Damn it, they should have checked with Rhiannon.

'Was, uhh, I need a... some pot?'

Nothing. The footy guys are still chasing each other; Robbo, from their English class, does a specky and the world doesn't end. There are no sirens, no alarms, Miss doesn't drop out of a gumtree to cart them off to Sir.

Autumn doesn't feel like any less of a good person for asking.

Sheridan makes a noise that's kind of caught in a knot between his mouth and his nose, a light gurgle. '*Pot?*'

It's work, not to ask him to keep his voice down. 'Y'know, marijuana. Specifically.'

Sheridan laughs. 'I know, *marijuana specifically*. It's just... funny.' He eyes Autumn more closely then, finally getting it. 'How old are you?'

'What's that got to do with anything?'

'Loads,' Sheridan says. He doesn't elaborate.

Autumn gives in. ''M'only a year below you.' Technically, this is true, as most of Autumn's classes are VCE Units 1 and 2.

Sheridan nods, shrugs, and his hands sink out of sight. Autumn can see the bulge of his phone in his pocket. 'All right, then.' He kicks off from the fence and trudges back up the oval.

Autumn spins around after him. 'Wait—'

But Sheridan just says, 'Not here.' He jerks his chin in the direction of the goal posts to where… Mrs Johnson is standing. Watching them.

Shit.

'Out front, at lunch. We'll go to my place.' Sheridan walks on ahead as if he's alone.

Now

People in movies always have crap in their lockers. Autumn has almost nothing. Their locker door is close to falling off, by the looks of it. They eye the silver snarl of a detached hinge up the back as Sir rips it further open. Inside, there are books because, umm, school. Some folders, a jumper, their last art assessment they've been meaning to take home but haven't, rolled up with a lacka band.

'Well-utilised I see,' Sir says, and it's gotta be sarcasm… right? Autumn isn't sure. Can principals even do that?

They nod anyway. It's not like they don't use their locker, or don't care, it's just that every time they open it, there's something weirdly satisfying about the absence in it, something about the hollowness and the assurance that Autumn doesn't *need* a lot in the first place, that they can survive *without*, that makes them want to scoop everything else out too. Make it entirely empty.

Sir reaches inside and gathers everything up in his arms: books, Autumn's jumper, their rolled artwork.

'Come with me, please,' he says, without looking back.

Autumn's gut drops to their toes.

They follow Sir to his office, where he asks them to sit down. Autumn does as Sir goes about the room, locking his door and adjusting the blinds till the sun is reduced to faint slits on the carpet. Autumn feels bad for his potted plants.

Pits and pores starting to gush, they sit and watch Sir sit too. He quietly begins to rummage about in their things, unrolling their artwork, smoothing it, unzipping zippers and turning pockets inside out.

Without looking up, he asks, 'Do you know what I'm looking for, Autumn?'

Yeah. 'No, sir.'

'Drugs,' he says.

Autumn shifts in their seat, placing their arms around their waist, at the bulge there. Their voice cracks. 'Sir?'

Sir says nothing, opening the small side pocket in Autumn's folder filled with slips of paper.

Autumn's temples throb, colour floods their face. 'I—I don't have, sir. I don't have—have anything.'

The way Sir looks at them is all brows.

They stew while he searches. Should they—what do liars sound like? Nervous? Scared? Confident in their innocence? Whichever way liars sound, Autumn wants to sound the opposite, but they can feel themself spiralling. Thighs squelching, sweaty on the seat beneath them, uncertainty stripping their confidence.

'We shall see.' Done with the things he collected from their locker, Sir extends one hand out for Autumn's backpack. 'I'm not… unsympathetic to the… rough time you're going through Autumn,' he begins as they hand it over and—

Nope. No. Autumn's got that GIF in their head of the octopus just bolting.

'I'm not going through anything, sir,' they cut in, looking at the blinds over Sir's shoulder. 'I'm fine.'

Sir doesn't even falter with the zipper, but he doesn't look up at them either. 'Yes. Well.'

Their backpack is almost Rob Liefeld-ian, having grown about a hundred pockets. Pens get spilled out across Sir's desk, scraps and folded paper, dried-up textas. Autumn's notes and notebooks get piled on top of one another. There's a charger cord, half-chewed headphones, and an old apple core. A bottomless backpack, a few minutes stretching out into a hundred hours. Autumn dies and lives and dies again, just them and Sir, whose expression sours as he turns the front pocket inside out.

Then

Autumn feels off about stepping out of school bounds and onto the footpath at lunch. Their hands won't stop shaking. The idea of their dad being called, told they left campus during school hours, Do not pass Go, Do not collect $200, is just not… no.

But Sheridan's already trotting up to them, *trotting*.

'C'mon,' he says, and starts off down the footpath.

Sheridan is casual, calm and collected. He walks with his

hands in his pockets, his bag off one shoulder. He's not the one making Autumn so nervous; they'd pay to have an ounce of that—that casual, calm collectedness. Their dad's always asking them why they're so stressed and strung-out, while Autumn keeps on thinking, well, how can I *not* be, with *everything*.

But they don't say so.

That'd make their dad feel worse.

Now

Autumn's drowning in their hoodie and jeans. Terror cools uncomfortably on their skin. They feel like crying, though it's not logical in cause or in function. Voice robbing, throat throbbing tears, the ones Autumn's swallowing down now, are prolactin, leu-enkephalin and adrenocorticotropic hormone. They're made up of endorphins, natural painkillers, and the same hormone that gets breasts working throughout pregnancy.

Sir lifts his eyes.

'Not today then, hmm?' he asks.

There's a try there for casualness, and Autumn goes to mimic. The room's kind of fuzzy, though, wobbling around the edges, so they settle for a safe, 'No, sir.'

Sir shifts through their things once again, sorting everything into little clumps on his desk. Their bag is empty, lifelessly draped over his lap.

'No idea?' he asks, gaze flicking down to their deflated backpack.

Autumn, unsure, shakes their head.

With a sigh, Sir sits forward, elbows planted on his desk, their faces now level.

'We have zero tolerance for drugs at this school,' he says. 'Zero. You are a student with a lot of potential, Autumn. You work hard, and the feedback I have received from your teachers is promising. You could go places.'

He says this as if there aren't already barriers in place for Autumn to get to the *places* they want to go. Why does he think they have to try so hard? Care so much?

'I am going to give you one final chance to tell me the truth. If you are honest, the consequences will be far less serious. If you lie to me—' his voice is deadly even in its severity '—I will be forced to act accordingly. Now, tell me the truth. Have you, now or ever, bought drugs from another student on school grounds?'

There's a scream clawing somewhere deep in Autumn's throat. They can see it, Dad called into school, slumped where they are now, witness to his kid getting tied up in cuffs or chains, his greatest fears, oh shit.

But still. Phrasing. Autumn holds on tight to their side and the bulge down by their waistband. 'No, sir.'

They do not move one iota until Sir tells them to collect their things and dismisses them.

Then

Sheridan's house is a *house*, firstly. Secondly, Sheridan has a rumpus room, a room that looks as though it hasn't seen any 'rumpussing' for a long time. The dartboard on the far wall is chalked up with scores, pool balls are arranged on the abandoned table like artefacts of some bygone game. Autumn can practically feel the dust throughout the whole house. It's weighed down by a skunky smell.

Sheridan's parents aren't home, but maybe if they were they'd be okay about their son selling drugs during school hours, maybe doing drugs, presumably? The smell?

God. 'I don't belong here,' Autumn says into the empty rumpus room.

Sheridan comes back into the room, a small sandwich baggie in hand. 'Oh-kay… ouch?' he says, having heard them. Shit.

'No, I'm just—' Autumn's fingers, flexing down by their sides as though grasping for words, finally spasm and curl tight around their bag straps. Specks of visible dust drift about, landing on Autumn's arms, their hoodie. They want to leave, there isn't… this isn't logical.

'I'm sorry, I should go.'

Yet even as they're saying this, they're stuck. Feet rooted in Newton's law. They stare at the baggie: weed's more *clumped* than they imagined, not that they really imagined, but it's just…

It's different. An actual plant, kinda, sorta. Not just some green mass on a screen.

'Did… you want me to stop you?' Sheridan asks, watching them watch him.

Autumn blinks. 'What?'

'From leaving.'

They don't know. They're not exactly leaving but they're not really doing much of anything else either. Is there enough in the bag? It looks like a lot, but then too little. God. Autumn's whole body is thrumming on a weird frequency.

'It's good,' Sheridan says, and the way he says it is kind, gentle. 'Promise.' It's like he's trying to coax an animal.

Autumn swallows down the urge to blurt, 'It's not for me.' Hands shaking, they reach into their bag, pull out their wallet. Sheridan steps forward.

'Deadpool?' he asks, looking down at Autumn's themed wallet. They got it for their birthday.

'Love it. Hey, you kinda look a bit like, what's her name, with the hair and the—'

Autumn knows. It's not a coincidence. 'Negasonic Teenage Warhead,' they say.

'Negasonic Teenage Warhead, fucken-A, yeah.' Sheridan clicks his fingers. His smile is so sweet, so gummy, stretching hard at the ties on either side that twist and pull in his mouth. Autumn throws their eyes to the floor. To their shoes. Which are boring. And kind of blurry.

Oh shit, wait—

A hand touches them. A soft, 'Hey, no, 's all right,' followed by an even softer, 'Crap, don't cry.'

Damn it. Autumn smears their sleeve across their face, dragging the back of their hand over their nose a couple of times. They scramble with their wallet. Get this over with. Get this done. Go home.

'W-Wasn't sure how much…'

'Hey, no, it's fine.' He isn't bothering to take it or count the notes Autumn's holding out. 'I get it.'

He doesn't really *get* it. At all. A part of Autumn is comforted, though, that he says he thinks he might. 'G-Got more—'

'No, it's fine.' This time, Sheridan steps back, putting distance between them. One corner of his mouth kicks up. 'First one's free.'

Autumn stands there, wallet out. 'Free?'

'Yeah.'

First of all, no. Secondly, *a)* No. *b)* No. They shake their head. 'I can't do that.'

Sheridan blinks. 'Oh-kay?'

'I mean it. Please.' There's a formula to this, a procedure. An exchange of goods for services. Autumn shoves the money at him. 'I'm not taking it if you're not too.'

In this school, this town, Autumn should be used to everyone knowing about their dad. Half the town works in the hospital after all. Even then, just for a second, they think maybe he doesn't know, that he's not going to say it. It's a thought as flimsy and thin as lined paper. Sheridan's words pinch either end and tear.

'It's not for you, though, right?' he asks without having to *really* ask. 'Your dad's—'

Something in Autumn's expression shutters him off.

'Hey, uh, shit.' Sheridan shifts from foot to foot. Not approaching, not backing off, some awkward middle ground. 'Sorry, it's just. Everyone sorta… knows, y'know? Small town—'

'How much?'

'Uh, just that he's sick—'

'No. How much for the bag?'

'I'm not gonna—'

'Please,' Autumn whispers, keeping their money outstretched.

Sheridan just stands there, and it's only when Autumn moves half a step forward, knuckles almost bumping his chest that he sighs, stepping back a bit. He takes the money. Some of the money. He curls the last twenty back under Autumn's fingers. Hands soft and warm.

'Next time,' he says. Because he *knows*.

Autumn sniffs and takes a second while Sheridan's back is turned, to make themself presentable. Too obvious in their pocket, they slide the baggie down into the waistband of their undies. Sheridan kicks off his shoes.

And whatever this is, it's done.

Now

Sometimes, when their dad looks tired, on the days when he can't get back to bed after dragging himself to the kitchen table, Autumn sits beside him, brings a book or a newspaper and asks him to read.

Their dad is good at reading, reads just about anything. Autumn loves the way his mouth forms the words, the gaps he takes between them, how his finger follows each mark on the page. He's good at reading and he's good at fixing. He fixed their house up before Autumn was born. He handwashes dishes, fixes torn shorts. He'd get up first when he used to work and fix Autumn some toast in the morning, turning the burnt bits delicious—an exact measured ratio of Vegemite and butter. He'd fix the car, the sink, the gutters, their neighbours' gutters, and even Autumn's phone when they dropped it.

The fern on the kitchen bench looks dead, but Autumn waters it, just in case. Dad should be up now, but he isn't. They throw down their bag, kick off their shoes, unravelling themself from everything that isn't here in this house. They pad down the hall in socks to their dad's room. They push on the door, fearing the worst.

Inside, heat presses down on them from all sides, even though there's a whirring fan in the corner. In bed, Dad's asleep, his thin frame outlined against sweat-soaked sheets.

He usually wakes up so easily: light, noise, anything.

'Dad?' Autumn puts a hand on his arm, not daring to squeeze, not wanting to hurt him. 'Dad?'

There's a long moment between that sleeping breath and the next one waking. Their dad shuffles over, one crusty eye sliding open before the other. 'Hey, Bub?' he whispers. Coughs phlegm that he doesn't even try to swallow, just turns his cheek into his pillow. 'How's school?'

'School's school,' Autumn answers, knowing he's not really hearing them. He's sunken so far into his pillows they're almost swallowing him. Dad's kind of looking at them, kind of up at the ceiling, his head sweaty and bare, greyish in the low light.

There's an irresistible urge then, inside Autumn, to cover him up, protect that vulnerability. Especially when their dad reaches out, hand blindly searching his bedside for his rolling papers.

Voice thick, eyes wet. Their dad looks at them. 'How was—' he breaks out into phlegmy coughs.

Autumn's hands sink into their waistband, where time and sweat and friggen Sir have fused plastic to their skin. Just a small bag. They're picking up some shifts next week and can pay Sheridan properly then, for this week's bag and next.

'Here, Dad.' They set it on his bedside.

Autumn knows pain isn't a feeling, not a feeling, really, just another chemical, able to be balanced when unbalanced. Nerve fibres and endorphins.

At first there's nothing, then recognition, then delight. Relief already in their dad's eyes.

'Bubba.' He moves too suddenly towards the baggie and is racked with rib-crushing coughs.

Autumn backs off, to help the pain, crossing their arms tight in front of themself. They watch their dad's probing fingers, his deep inhale as he lifts them from the baggie to his nose. The longing stare, his smile. Oxytocin.

'Beautiful, Bub. You legend.'

'Yeah-nah, all right.'

Dad reaches out for their hand. 'Beautiful.' His hand trembles, but it always trembles. Autumn sits again, watching their dad sit up. Soon, arid smoke lifts up and swirls around Autumn, blown by the fan across the room.

'God.' Dad breathes out a dragon's breath. After a few minutes, the line of his shoulders has eased. He's not a patient, a burden, their sick dad. He's a guy in bed, and tonight, tomorrow, he might actually be able to get out of it.

He looks up at them, and that look evolves into a weary smile.

'C'mere.' Autumn dives forward. '*Mmmpfh.*'

Arms tight around his neck, a flame too close to their head. But they don't care. They always hug. They're a hugging family. This time, Autumn hugs him a little more. Feels the outline of him under thin skin and cloth. The shape of a benzene molecule.

'Wasn't any trouble?' he asks them without really asking, his momentarily pain-free, lucid mind already on other things.

'Nah. No trouble.'

Their dad puts his arms around them, Autumn curls inward. Warm and alive.

After a while he whispers, 'Think you might be bruising me, Bub.' He laughs, then coughs.

So, Autumn lets him go.

The Bees

BY
STACEY MALACARI

The bees went first. Great swarms blanketed the whole of Perth city for three days, frantically searching every tree, every flower, for one last chance at survival. The buzz was like an alarm clock jammed inside my brain. On the fourth day, the buzzing stopped. All that was left of the bees were empty hives and thousands of fuzzy carcasses covering the streets. The buzzing was replaced with a crunching sound as people marched into their workplaces, still pretending that global warming wasn't real, that the sea levels weren't rising, and that the city wouldn't be completely underwater in a month's time. The coastal suburbs were already half submerged by then. At least one multimillion-dollar beach house sank into the ocean each day, like it was nothing more than a sandcastle. But the clocks kept ticking and the cogs kept turning.

When the Swan River finally broke its banks, the flood water raced along St Georges Terrace, up William Street, spilling across Yagan Square, dripping into the underground rail, turning the South Perth foreshore into a swamp. The government finally sounded the alarm—a constant beep emitted from speakers bolted to the roofs of all the skyscrapers— and started herding us all out of the city, setting up a refugee camp above the coastal plain.

That was my seventeenth birthday.

They cut the power two days after that, hoping to force stragglers like us out. A lot of people wouldn't—or couldn't—go. They sent buses around to transport anyone who couldn't make their own way out, but they didn't send enough, and they didn't send them to the right places, as usual. We could have left well before they cut the power, but Mum refused. She kept telling me, 'We'll go tomorrow,' and then she'd go off to her room with a bottle of wine and disappear until morning. The next day she'd say the same thing.

I was up early on the day we finally left. It was the day after they cut the power. The light was still grey. The breeze coming through the open windows of our house was cool, despite the summer heat wave. The air had already turned sour by then, but first thing in the morning it wasn't so bad. I wore socks that day, ones with a pattern of the moon and the words 'It's Just a Phase' printed on them. Mum was in the kitchen. I could hear her talking to someone. I paused in the hallway, hidden from view, and peered around the corner. Mum sat at the old wooden table, phone to her ear. I ducked back behind the wall and crouched on the floor, listening.

'Enough is enough, Mum,' she said. She was speaking to Nan. 'I've organised for the bus to collect you today at noon. The water is getting higher, this is the last chance you'll have.' There was the sound of a metal spoon being stirred in a ceramic mug, despite the hot water being out. She was drinking her coffee cold.

She let out a long sigh. I could imagine her with her head in her hands, rubbing at her temples, the way I'd seen her do a thousand times—particularly when she was on the phone to Nan.

'Honestly? No, I don't really care whether you come or stay. But Remi does,' said Mum. 'Are you at least going to say goodbye to her? I'm used to you pissing off and only thinking about yourself, but she still thinks the world of you, not that you deserve it.'

A pause. I heard Mum take a sip of coffee as she listened to Nan's response.

'No, she's still asleep,' said Mum. 'I'll get her to call you when she's— What do you mean, "no"? You have to say goodbye.'

Mum was breathing heavy. The chair scraped again. I could hear her footsteps on the floorboards, pacing around the kitchen. I stayed frozen, staring at my socks.

'Don't give me that crap,' Mum said to Nan. 'You know she won't accept that. If you don't say goodbye, you know exactly what she's going to do. Is that what you want?'

Mum was hurling dishes into the sink. She always made a lot of noise when she was pissed off.

'You know what, don't even bother with your excuses. I'm so done with all this. Stay there and die alone for all I care. I was fine without you when you left me and Dad to run away with May. I was fine without you when the kids were born. I was— No, you listen to me! I was fine without you when Joe died. I've been fine without you my whole life and I'll be fine without you now. I'll sleep soundly at night knowing you can never bother me ever again. As for Remi, I'll tell her the bus came to collect you, but it was too late, you were already dead.'

I couldn't stand what I was hearing. Mum wasn't even trying to convince Nan to come with us. She was such a hypocrite, calling Nan out for being a shitty parent. When I'd come out as gay to Mum she'd all but kicked me out of the house. She told me I could do whatever I wanted, just as long as it wasn't under her roof. I'd called Nan straight away and she'd welcomed me with open arms. Nan was there for me, no question. At least she was, until Nana May died, then it all became too hard. I ended up back at Mum's, but it was never the same. I got that Nan coming out and abandoning her and Grandad really did a number on Mum. I got that, I did, but how was that my fault? Why did I have to suppress who I was just because Mum hadn't dealt with her own shit?

I heard Mum open the fridge, then the distinct *hiss… clunk* of a beer bottle being opened and placed on the table. Cold coffee, warm beer. 'Whatever,' said Mum, the fight gone from her voice. I heard her throw down the phone.

I felt the tension in my body reach breaking point. My skin was burning, my fists clenched so hard they hurt. My breathing was hard, so hard I was sure Mum must have heard me there long before I burst into the room, ready for a fight.

'What the fuck do you think you're doing?' I screamed at Mum. 'You're just going to leave her to die?'

She barely flinched. Her hat was pulled down low over her eyes and her hands were shaking as she held the beer. She looked up at me slowly, then pushed the beer away.

'Don't start, Remi.'

'We have to go get her.'

'What do you want me to say? She doesn't want to leave,' said Mum, pushing her hat off and then putting it back on. Nothing I could say would get through to her. I swung out and punched the back of the dining chair closest to me.

'Grow up,' spat Mum, not even looking at me.

'I'm going to get her,' I yelled. My whole body was alight. I felt strong, like I could pick up the table and throw it across the room if I wanted to. That's when Frida, my baby sister, just four months old, started crying. I don't know if that's the only reason I didn't start throwing the furniture around, but it sucked some of the intensity out of me. Mum looked up at me, eyes blank. Then she sighed and pushed herself up from the chair. She walked right by me without a word and went into Frida's room.

I took out my phone and dialled Nan's number. It went to voicemail. I tried again. Voicemail. I snatched Mum's car keys from the bench.

I loaded up the car in a fit of anger, grabbing anything I thought might be useful, which turned out to be a whole lot of shit that wouldn't be. I was putting the last bag in when Mum followed me out holding Frida, who was still screaming her lungs out.

'Where do you think you're going?' said Mum.

'I told you. To get Nan. You coming or what?'

Mum stared at me a minute, blinking too slow. I was prepared for a battle, prepared to argue with her and force her in the car if I had to. I was stronger than her. But she just looked at me from under that old red hat and said, 'Fine.'

'What do you mean, "fine"?'

'I mean, I'm done fighting with you, Rem. If you want to be selfish and take our only means of transport and drag Frida through the flood, only to hear in person what you already know to be true, so be it. We'll go.'

That made my stomach twist. I hadn't considered Frida. But it would literally take an extra hour, max, to pick up Nan first. Plenty of time. I took Frida from Mum and gave her a big kiss. Mum rummaged through Frida's baby bag and scooped the last of the formula into a bottle. She handed it to me.

'Ration it,' she said. 'I'll drive.'

I strapped Frida into her car seat while Mum finished loading the car. Frida and I sat side by side in the back, and I dangled an owl toy in her face to distract her from her hunger. The owl had crunchy ribbons to touch, bells to jingle, and a little mirror that Frida liked to look at and then look behind to try and find the baby she saw reflected there, not understanding that it was her. She was content for a few minutes, her tiny hands grabbing at the owl, but then she spotted the cold bottle of formula in my hand and screamed again. Mum slid into the driver's seat and turned on the car.

'Just a little bit of milk at a time. We'll get more at the camp,' said Mum, without looking back.

I held the bottle to Frida's lips and she drank greedily. As soon as I pulled the bottle away she began to scream again. I stuck a half-chewed rusk stick in her mouth, but she kept on screaming, tiny fists banging against the sides of the car seat.

'It's okay, little boo, you can have some more milk soon, *shh, shh*,' I cooed, but that only made her scream louder.

'Frida, baby, nice and quiet for Mummy now, come on, baby,' said Mum as she pulled out of the driveway.

Frida was not nice and quiet, but at least her cries drowned out the sound of the evacuation alarm. The *beep, beep, beep* had mostly faded into the background by then, but on my bad days it was all I could hear. It drove me crazy.

'Fuck this,' Mum muttered to herself. 'Fuck all of this.'

I sang *Twinkle, Twinkle, Little Star* to Frida to drown out Mum. I tightened the cap on the bottle so that hardly any milk came out when Frida sucked, then gave it back to her to nurse. She wasn't happy, but stopped screaming long enough for us to get out of the estate.

'She'll sleep soon,' Mum said to herself again. 'Everything will be fine, she'll sleep.'

A few of our neighbours left at the same time as us. I watched them through the window as we passed. Some looked completely traumatised at the thought of leaving their precious bricks and mortar behind, others—renters like us, I supposed—barely glanced back as they loaded their photo albums and clothes into their cars. The radio was repeating the emergency broadcast, telling us where to go and what to bring and how far the flood waters had reached.

Frida started screaming again five minutes onto the highway. We'd just passed the turnoff for the airport, the traffic backed up as far as I could see, people desperate to get out, even though a ticket to anywhere cost more than a house by then. That's when I realised we were going the wrong way.

'Turn around, Mum.'

Mum pressed her lips together, her knuckles white on the steering wheel. 'No.'

'We're not leaving without Nan.'

'She doesn't want to leave.'

'She wouldn't let me leave without saying goodbye!' I yelled. 'We have to go back for her. She's all alone.' I unbuckled my seatbelt, knocking Frida's owl to the floor. The car started beeping, telling me to put my seatbelt back on. Frida started screaming again.

Mum slammed on the brakes. 'Put your seatbelt back on, Remi. I'm not doing this with you. She doesn't want to leave. All your nan cares about is herself, that's all she's ever cared about. You're better off forgetting about her. She sure doesn't give a shit about us!'

Parents are usually right, but in this case, Mum was wrong.

I took advantage of the car being stopped, grabbed my backpack, yanked open the door, and jumped out.

'You get your arse back in this car right now!' Mum was pissed. Frida was pissed. I was pissed.

I slammed the door shut. Mum pulled the car onto the shoulder of the highway, cutting off my escape route. She got out of the car, face red, tears streaming down her cheeks. That made me stop. Mum and I fought all the time, but there were only three times I'd seen her cry: when my brother Joe died; when her dad died; and when she found out she was pregnant with Frida.

'You can't stop me,' I said.

Mum ran her hands over her face. Inside the car, Frida was still bawling.

'Remi, please, baby, I know I sound harsh, but you don't know her like I do. You can plead and cry at her feet until your throat is raw, she won't budge.'

'Yes, she will. If I ask her to come, she will, I know it. Let's just turn around, throw Nan in the car, then head for the camp. What's the big deal?'

Mum looked me dead in the eye, her patience for me gone. 'What's the big deal?' She grabbed me around the wrist. 'What's the big fucking deal, Remi? The big deal is that you are not the only person in this family, mate. Look around you! Frida is in there screaming her lungs out because she's starving. I'm exhausted. Yet all you care about is Nan.' She was crying hard then, almost as hard as Frida. She let go of my wrist, leaving a red mark behind. She dropped to her knees on the bitumen and looked up into the sky.

'Mum,' I said. I reached out a hand to touch her, but she batted it away. I softened my voice. 'Mum, you know how much she means to me. I care about Frida too, and you, but I need to say goodbye.'

After a moment, she let out a sigh, wiped her tears on her sleeve. She stood up again. Mum never let herself appear weak for long. 'I'm sorry, baby, I really am. I know I've not been the greatest mum, but at least I'm here. Your nan has made her decision. I know you love her, but there is no way in hell I am going to let you just fuck off into this flood and risk losing you, too.'

I didn't know how to tell her I was going whether she 'let' me or not.

Mum must have read it in my face. 'You're going to go anyway, aren't you?'

I nodded. 'Sorry, Mum.'

'You're just like her, you know,' she said, and she was right. 'Stubborn as all hell.'

'I know we don't have the tightest of relationships, Mum, but you know I love you, right?' My feet were bouncing back and forth, my mind already plotting how to get to Nan.

Mum pulled me into a hug. It felt weird hugging her. We never really did that.

'I'm not sure why you love me,' she said.

'Mum, come on, don't do this.'

'I love you too, Rem,' she said. 'I really do.'

'All right, Mum, let's not get too emo. Let's just go already.'

Mum looked over at the car. Frida had fallen asleep, exhausted from all the screaming. 'We can't, babe,' she said. 'I have to get Frida to the camp or she'll…'

'Yeah, I know. It's cool, I can take care of myself.'

'I know you can,' said Mum, a sad look in her eye, the look I couldn't stand because it made me feel sorry for her, even though I was still so mad at her. 'Promise me you'll come straight to the camp after.'

'Promise. Everything except the "straight" part.'

That almost made Mum smile.

'You know where the camp is, right?' she said, ignoring my joke.

'Yes, Mum.' I rolled my eyes. Now she cared.

'And you know how to get there?'

'Yes, Mum.'

'How are you going to get there?'

'I dunno, steal a car or something, I guess?'

That time, Mum rolled her eyes at me. 'Do you have water?'

'Yes, Mum. I won't be long, like a few hours, max.'

'You call me if you get into trouble, you understand? How much battery does your phone have left?'

'Heaps, Mum, just get Frida there safely and don't worry about me. I'll be fine.'

Mum stared at me for an uncomfortably long time. 'All right,' she said. 'Fuck off, then.'

I gave her a nod, then ducked back into the car to kiss Frida goodbye, breathing in her newborn baby smell. She looked so cute when she was asleep, with her tiny fingers and her squishy cheeks. I had to pretend she was just on her way to daycare or something, because the thought of my little sister heading off to a refugee camp made my stomach turn.

Mum got back in the car and pulled out onto the road. I didn't watch them leave. I'd been on my own before, and even though it didn't feel like I would be fine, I had to tell myself I'd be fine, or I wouldn't have been able to keep going.

We had travelled far enough east that the ground was still dry. Nan lived just north of the city, a twenty-minute drive from where I stood on the side of the highway, but I had no ride, and the temperature was close to forty degrees. I debated hitchhiking, versus walking, versus stealing a car. The decision wasn't hard, because I hate random people, and the heat and I are not friends.

I ducked through the scrubland on the side of the highway and made my way down into the adjacent suburb. Nice houses, dead lawns, just like all the new estates, ours included. I had to try three cars before I found one unlocked. Stealing, I felt okay about. Smashing windows, not so much. I never really thought of myself as a criminal, but it was surprisingly easy to be okay with stealing a car when your entire city was about to be annihilated. Was that how it always began? The looting and shit that went on in situations like this? What would you do if you knew you could get away with it?

I'd lied to Mum when I said I had heaps of battery left. It was really freaking hard to keep a charged phone when there was no power. I was down to 20%. With 3% of that, I googled how to hot-wire a car. I spent twenty minutes trying to find the wires to hot-wire. Failed. I googled some more, sweating like I'd just eaten ten ghost chillies. I was getting nowhere, when some chick came out of the house opposite, wearing shorts and a singlet, hair up in a bun. She checked both ways, then crossed the street to me.

'Trying to steal a car, hey?' she said.

'Who, me?' I said, trying to be cool, but failing, because yes, I was stealing a car, and the chick was kinda hot.

'Nah, the person beside you.'

I looked beside me without thinking. 'Oh. That was dumb,' I said to my shoes.

She laughed, then chucked me a set of keys. 'We have two cars. Can only take one with us. You can use the other. But it better be for something good.'

I stood there, silently staring down at the keys, wondering what the catch was.

'So, is it for something good?' she asked.

'Gotta go rescue my nan.'

The chick smiled and nodded. 'Better get on with it then. Whole fucking place will be underwater soon, and I don't have a boat you can steal.' She turned and pointed at a white car parked across the road. 'Drive safe.'

She started back across the street.

'Uh, thanks?' I called after her.

'Don't mention it,' she said, before disappearing back inside her house.

I drove with the sinking sun in my eyes. At that time of the day, the highway would usually be bumper to bumper. Peak hour. But all the traffic was headed in the opposite direction. It was just me on my side of the road. If I ignored the traffic jam on the other side of the highway, I could pretend I was someplace else, cruising up toward Ningaloo, summer road trip, care-free.

If only.

I tried not to think about Mum and Frida. They would be fine. Everything would be fine. I'd see them soon, no worries. Just had to find Nan, convince her to come with me, then we'd get out of there and make our way to the camp. Easy.

I put all thoughts of them out of my mind and focused on the car instead. I tried to guess what kind of person the chick who owned it was. The kind of person who gave away her car, obviously, but people did weird things when the world was ending. There was nothing much in the car other than a half-empty bottle of water and a completely empty bag of Macca's. That made me hungry. The car smelled nice, like vanilla, and there was a *Jack's Mannequin* CD in the stereo. I turned up 'Swim' and enjoyed the irony and nostalgia of the song.

~

I parked outside Nan's apartment block, the water already a couple of centimetres up my tyres. The water was still slow-moving, seeping into all the cracks and crevices first, filling the stormwater drains and the channels people had dug in their front lawns, but I was cutting it fine with this visit.

The building was one of those ancient, ugly, brick blocks—a sky-high eyesore. It looked abandoned, the gates wide open, the smell of decay and waste already thick in the air. Two dead cats and a dog had been left by the bin. I shoved my shirt over my nose, but that didn't keep the stench out.

I took the stairs two at a time, having to jump over a dead body on the flight just before Nan's floor. I tried not to think of it as a body. I imagined it as a pile of laundry instead, abandoned by some careless resident as they prepared to evacuate, the bundle too heavy and mundane to bother with. That's all it was. Just clothes.

I found Nan's front door open. From where I stood out on the landing, I could see her on her balcony, seven stories up, watching the flood rise. I stepped softly into the apartment. There were no sounds except the evacuation alarm from the city, louder here than at home. I didn't know how Nan could stand it. She was in her favourite chair, where she sat every day to watch the sunset. The light that evening made her look both very young and very old at the same time. She was eating a pear, one slice at a time, like it was just an ordinary day. There used to be birds there, magpies and kookaburras, that would land on the railing and sing their songs. Now there was just

Nan, her pear, and the incoming flood.

'Nan, it's me,' I said.

She coughed, but didn't turn around. I took a few more steps into the darkness of the apartment and waited. Had she heard me? I didn't want to startle her. I was about to call out again when she finally spoke.

'If the world ended today, would you die happy?'

I stood, frozen, not sure how to answer.

'Well, Remi? Would you?' She turned to face me, one eyebrow raised in that old, familiar way.

'Asking the hard questions there, Nan. I'm not sure,' I said. 'I guess not.'

'Then you better get out of here, missy.'

'Come with me, Nan. I have a car, we can make it to the camp, easy as. Mum and Frida are already on their way.'

Nan bit another slice of pear, the second-last one, but said nothing. I could see her mind ticking over, collecting her words carefully, the way she always did. I looked around the apartment as I waited. All she had was a bed, a chair, her writing desk, and her books—hundreds of books. She had photos of our family tucked inside the pages as bookmarks, the edges frayed and faded. There was a copy of *The Handmaid's Tale* on the kitchen bench, stuffed with photos. My heart sank at that. That was for me. I knew it.

Without the reading lamp glowing in the corner, or the radio humming those old songs she loved, the apartment seemed more like a time capsule than a home. It still smelled like her, but the scent was fading, being replaced by the scent of the flood: empty buildings, stagnant drains, abandoned pets, burning piles of garbage from the eastern suburbs—the last-ditch attempt of some batshit mayor to save their town from inevitable diseases.

'You're making me nervous lurking about in the shadows like that, Remi Marie. Come and sit down,' said Nan, waving her hand at the seat beside her.

I sat next to Nan on the balcony, sweat instantly pooling under my thighs. From up there, the water looked calm. Beautiful, even. It reflected the light of the setting sun, orange glints like sparks from a fire. Nan finished her pear and reached across the table for her pouch of tobacco. She slid it across to me. I took out the papers, filters and the last of the tobacco, and rolled her final cigarette. I had been rolling Nan's cigarettes ever since the arthritis had stopped her being able to do it herself. I passed the smoke to her and flicked open her old lighter, the one Nana May had given her on their third date. I used to tease Nana May that giving a girl a lighter wasn't very romantic, and she'd always reply, 'Might not be romantic, but it certainly started a fire.' Then she and Nan would give each other a look and laugh at the memory, still so in love with each other after all those years. I always wanted a love like my grandmothers shared.

Nan took a drag of the cigarette, trails of grey smoke winding up into the darkening sky, filling the air with that sweet scent that reminded me of her whenever I smelled it.

'Were you really not going to say goodbye to me?' I said. My voice cracked. I felt the sour saltiness of tears in the back of my throat.

'Remi,' said Nan. There was pity in her voice. I hated that. 'I have never needed anyone to save me before, why start now? I knew if you found out I wasn't coming you'd do something stupid like this. I love you dearly, but if I die now, I die happy. Alone.'

She passed me the cigarette. I took a drag. Although I didn't really like smoking, I liked being connected to Nan in that way. I felt the tears hit my cheeks before I even registered that I was crying. Nan glanced over as she plucked the cigarette back from me, then returned her gaze to the city. All the windows of the skyscrapers were dark. The trees were still. We watched the final rays of light drop away below the horizon.

'Take the photos. And the book. Don't look back,' she said.

'Nan, I…' But I trailed off. There was nothing I could say. She was leaving me. Again.

Nan turned to face me, grey eyes staring deep into mine. I felt myself unravelling. She scooped my hands up, so that they were cocooned inside hers. The cigarette hung from her lip. She pulled me in close, my ear to her chest. I breathed in her scent of tea tree and smoke, fabric softener and skin.

'Don't leave me,' I cried into her, my voice muffled by the thick sweater she was wearing, despite it still being at least thirty degrees out.

'I'm sorry,' said Nan. 'I love you, Rem. I really do. But Frida needs you. Your mother needs you. You have to go. Leave an old lady to die in peace, would you? Goodbye, Rem. You'll always be my girl.'

That hit me like a fist. The tears flowed. She kissed me on the head, and I knew from the way her kiss spread through my entire body, right to the core of my soul, that that kiss was the last thing she would allow us to share.

I ripped my hands out of hers, wanting her to know I was angry, but scared to let go all the same. I forced myself to stand, hoping she'd pull me back down, but she didn't. I stumbled from the balcony toward the front door.

I scooped the book and photos from the kitchen bench, my body going through the motions of walking, with no conscious effort from my brain. All I could think of was Nan, and the pear, and how she would die there alone. Happily. My brain flicked back and forth between feeling sorry for myself and feeling mad as hell at Nan. How could she do this to me again?

I refused to look back at Nan as I left the apartment, not even after I heard the *click, click, click* of her struggling with the lighter. If I had, I probably would have tried to drag her frail old body from that stupid apartment, down the stairs and out to the car, driven her across the floodwaters to the camps and forced her to sit in the corner with her impractical jumper and her empty pouch of tobacco and live on like the rest of us. But I had to leave her there, as much as it killed me, and there was no way in hell I would have gotten her down those stairs. I had to keep going, for Frida's sake, if nothing else. I needed Nan, but Frida needed me more.

I slammed Nan's door shut behind me, then sank a punch right next to the rusted number 58. She must have heard it, but I didn't give a shit at that point. The tears were streaming down my face, my cheeks burning, my throat feeling like it had closed over, but I let out a scream so loud that if Nan hadn't heard the punch to her door, she sure as hell would have heard that. I wanted her to come out. I waited on the landing for what seemed like hours, body trembling, staring hard at that door, willing it to open and for Nan to appear, bag in hand. I imagined her saying, 'All right, no need to throw a tantrum. Let's get on with it then.'

But she didn't. The door stayed shut. I attempted to punch the door again, but my arms were limp. I felt all the fight leave my body. I looked down at the book and the pictures of us and considered throwing them both off the landing.

I whispered my final goodbye to her, then turned and walked away.

It happened on the way down.

The bundle of laundry that wasn't a bundle of laundry at all. I tripped, leaving one Converse lodged squarely in its armpit and the rest of my body catching air. The book and the photos were flung from my hand. Pictures of me and Nan fluttered above my head as I fell. I reached out to try and stop myself, but there was nothing to hold onto.

It wasn't like my life flashed before my eyes so much. Just thoughts. Flashes of regrets. I thought about Mum, doing the best she could with the shit hand she'd been dealt. I thought about Frida, born into a world that didn't give a fuck about her. She wouldn't remember me. She wouldn't remember all the nappies I changed for her, or the bottles, or the songs, or the stories, or the hours I spent rocking her to sleep when she was starving. But I would never forget her. I thought about the chick who gave me her car. I didn't even ask her name. I thought of Nan and hoped to hell that she never left that apartment, because if she did she would find me obliterated at the bottom of her stairwell.

My world ended that day, but did I die happy? As the concrete rushed up to meet me, I was reminded of the bees, how they must have seen a similar final image as they fell from the sky. That was my parting thought. The bees went first.

The Gap Between Us

BY

SOFIA CASANOVA

Mum gave me this book on space when I was ten. The pages were deckled and there were pop-ups—ten-year-old me was easy to please.

One afternoon, after sunbathing with our Labrador, Cleo, I decided that painting my room with a can of glow-in-the-dark paint was a good idea. I saw it in the garage in the corner, just waiting to be touched. I didn't use a brush because my hands were so much better. I smeared stars and moons and planets; they had their own solar systems, moons gravitating around them, and black holes didn't exist on my map. Why would I want something on my wall that literally inhaled light?

When Mum came home, exhausted, I showed her my artistic masterpiece. She dropped her grocery bags at the sight.

I slept in my parents' bed that night, the paint fumes tickling my nose, thinking about Saturn and its moons, about how I couldn't see the stars in Strathfield.

I see them now. Those giant balls of plasma that hold people's hopes, dreams and wishes. The same globes of light that decide our fate. It's kind of silly how much faith we have in them; we believe the stars listen to us when humanity is but a tiny speck in the midnight fabric of the universe.

Isn't that kind of tragic? Can stars pay our bills? Because if I had a dollar for every time I'd seen a Southern Cross tattoo on someone, I'd be able to afford that 3D pen I've been eyeing off for a while.

At the end of the day, they're giant balls of plasma, not miracle workers.

This is what I'm thinking about as my panic attack dies away; my lungs start to open up as my eyes stay glued to the spaces between the pinpricks of thousands-of-years-old light. I'm lying on the bonnet of Liz's 1996 Toyota Corolla in the middle of the Great Ocean Road. Ironically, I can't smell the ocean from where we're parked. I used to think the whole road was a long journey of sea salt, flowers and sun-bleached hair. How wrong I was.

After the tyre popped and I almost lost my composure, we had to roll the car off the road slowly so we didn't lose the entire wheel. We were on the way to see the Loch Ard Gorge. Liz was giddy, ready to skinny dip and vlog as soon as we got there. It was 2:04 p.m. when I felt it: a sudden bump as Liz turned a sharp corner. The scent of burnt rubber filled the car and I was on the edge of my seat, gripping the dashboard.

'LIZ, WHAT IS THAT?'

She pulled over and dropped her head onto the steering wheel.

'For fuck's sake, we popped a tyre.'

We were lucky to be close enough to a rest area. Liz decided to change the tyre in the morning. She popped open a couple of Coronas that we kept in an esky in the boot, and made us ham and cheese sandwiches for dinner.

I didn't see it coming, the sudden wave of *everything*. Popping a tyre isn't that big a deal; yet my head blew the fact up so big I nearly fainted from the stress and tightness in my chest. Funny how anxiety works like that.

Liz is pulling out a blanket from the backseat and I'm holding my coin between my fingers, trying to find some sense of calm in the engravings on the metal. The rim of the metal feels like stuttered breaths against my skin, like what I was feeling a few minutes ago. It's an old Australian penny, a gift from my old art teacher. Maybe it's the copper hues or the fact it's still around after all these years that grounds me when I touch it.

Liz places the blanket on my feet and climbs onto her car, sitting next to me. She wraps the blanket around my legs, sure to cover my exposed feet, and pulls out her phone.

'Here, I saved this for when you're feeling like the world is on tilt.'

It's a video of Cleo wagging her tail and refusing to play fetch with Liz. I hear my voice encouraging Cleo to run after the stick, yet she's rooted to the spot, loving Liz scratching her behind the ear. And I have to be honest, it lifts the weight in my chest a little.

Liz quickly checks her Twitter notifications, then slips the phone into her pocket.

I hear the rush of the sea and try to imagine the sea spray

like tiny diamonds suspended in the night, the salt coating the rocks, the creatures beneath hunting and *living*. It takes me a second to notice the heaviness is fading. I can feel my body on the bonnet, the heat of the car receding second by second. I'm glad Liz remembered to turn the car off. Petrol prices are high enough as is, and we aren't exactly rolling in money.

'I don't know why they don't understand that on some days, your mind isn't your friend. And that you need your meds.' Liz's voice is a knife in the dark, one that misses my heart, yet manages to dig into my ribs. I know how she feels about this, about what happened back home. About the tension I left behind. 'This never happened with mine.'

I shrug. 'I'll handle it.' When I go back. *If* I go back.

I want to remind her she's also leaving, removing herself from the *Lucy + Liz = Friends Till Death* equation because reality has gotten in the way. But I don't.

She gives me a withering look, one that I know too well. With a sigh, she wraps the blanket around us, pulls a cigarette out of her pocket and lights it up. We share the smoke until it's nothing but ash between our fingers. Mum would kill me if she saw me like this.

'So what happens in the next update?'

'Well…' Liz loves spoilers so I tend to indulge her. 'Kelsey and Jane are on a date at the beach. There will definitely be a kiss.' My fingers itch to draw on my Wacom— I left it at home to keep it safe. 'Kelsey and Jane are living my best life. It'll be the fluffiest update in a while.'

'*Eeeeee*! So excited.' Liz grins and scrunches her nose with glee. 'Yours is the only comic I read.'

I'm glad the darkness is hiding my burning cheeks. 'I know.'

'Well, we're not going anywhere for a while so get comfy, honey.' Liz drags me into the car where she's pushed the seats down so they're like stretchers. She reaches over us to grab the pillows from the backseat, tucking one under my head. We lie together, gazing up at people's hopes and dreams through the windscreen, utterly silent, bar the earbuds in each of our ears. I think about Kelsey and Jane, about their future date, their first kiss, their everything. Will they be happy? That's up to me, I guess. The thousands of Tumblr followers who religiously reblog my comic with comments like 'MAKE THEM KISS' seem to know they're bound to last forever.

But will I be happy? Because I won't last forever.

I wanted to run away from home a lot as a kid. Mum said I was too sensitive to everything, and that I needed to not take things personally. Perhaps they were the childish fantasies of a girl who hated school and was overshadowed by an overachieving brother. I used to open the trip planner for Sydney Trains and a timetable for a country train to the Central Coast or Goulburn. I'd bring Liz with me, of course. I couldn't run away solo. Where I go, she goes. Where she goes, I go.

It was Liz's idea to leave, to make it an adventure. Her parents bought her the Corolla as a present for being the first person in her family to finish high school, without realising she'd be going overseas a year later. Feeling quite indebted and guilty, she wanted to use it as much as possible. *Really* give it a whirl before flying away from home—from *me*.

'So I'm thinking of driving along the Great Ocean Road. I mean—' she showed me a vlog on her phone of someone's trip around Victoria '—doesn't it look so *lush*? Absolutely perfect for my channel.'

'Yes, *ma'am*. When, though?' My eyes were glued to the rapid footage of trees, clear blue sea, and photogenic sunsets. And the smiles.

She flopped onto my bed, silver hair curling around her round face. 'When you finish exams.'

'I might not even pass my exams.' My stomach clenched with unease, and a sour taste climbed up my throat. 'I didn't think economics would be this mind-numbing.'

'So you hate it?'

'I never said that.'

'You *do* hate it!' A smile tugged on her lips. 'I told you. Business and all that shit, it isn't for you. That's more your parents. You can do whatever you want.'

I sat at my desk, stacks and stacks of notes either side of me. Colour-coordinated, categorised by chapter, and covered in doodles of Kelsey and Jane. A scene for their comic I was working on was visible on my Wacom, my digital art tablet. I'd turned off my desktop to deter myself from getting distracted, but I wanted to get the setting right for their kiss.

Liz took my silence as a cue to continue. 'I just can't imagine you in a pantsuit working in a high-rise building in a cubicle. I see you in sweatpants with art everywhere. Like your room!' She gestured to the various prints I had blu-tacked to my walls, mostly landscape digital art or Studio Ghibli fanart. 'Also, are you taking your meds?'

I hesitated, then said, 'Mum said I don't need them.'

Liz tried to catch my fleeting gaze. I focused on the stationery on my desk, the pastel pens suddenly so intriguing… and not in their colour-coded sections.

'Fuck it, Lien. Let's just go now!'

I whirled on her, heart thundering, palms already clammy, the fear of failure looming. She had to be joking. There was no way she was suggesting I simply drop everything and leave? Yet I looked at her and she was serious—her face was split into a grin, excited energy radiating from her.

And the crazy thing is, I agreed.

So naturally, I told my parents I was going away for a while in a text message—the classy way to do it—flipped my middle finger at my brother's bedroom door on my way out, and hopped into Liz's car. I haven't turned my phone on since then.

The sky is satin-pink and fluffy with clouds when I wake. For a second, I wish I hadn't woken up, yet I immediately reach for my phone and turn it on to check Tumblr. It takes me a second to realise I've made a big mistake.

20 missed calls from *Mum*.

12 missed calls from *Bro*.

15 voice messages.

Texts from both Mum and Dad buzz on my lock screen.

> *Dad*   *4 hrs ago*
> *iMessage*
> When are you coming home?

> *Dad*   *3 hrs ago*
> *iMessage*
> Darling, let us know where you are
> and how you're going.

> *Mum*   *1 hr ago*
> *iMessage*
> Lien call us please.

'Shit.' My phone is on 2%.

I'm cranky, my neck is stiff, and Liz has been farting all night. I get out of the car and sit on the bonnet. The summer heat hasn't quite reached its peak, but despite being parked in the shade of large trees, the metal beneath me won't stay cool for long.

I take the plunge and call Mum. Whatever happens is Future Lucy's problem. I find my coin in my pocket and run my thumb over the familiar metal.

The dial tone rings, and rings, and rings.

It's 10:07 a.m. She should be awake.

I check my phone: 1%.

'Lien!' She sounds… relieved?

The phone sticks to my sweaty palms. 'Hi, Mum.'

'Are you okay?' She's speaking Vietnamese. She's stressed.

'Yeah.'

She breathes into the receiver, a husky crackle coming through. 'Good, good. When are you coming home? There's a letter from the university. They said you have withdrawn. We can talk when you get home.'

Something twists in my chest. 'Why did you open my mail?' My phone makes a noise—that's never a good sign. 'Mum, my phone is about to die. Can I call you later?'

'What do you mean about to die? Why can't you talk to me now?'

'Mum, I have no battery! I'll call you—'

Oh shit, it's dead. I pocket the phone, staring at the black screen, resigned to the fact that they know now. It's rather deflating. I go to the boot to find the bag of apples we brought with us. They're bruised from Liz's insane driving. I find the one with the least damage, sit on the guardrail facing the ocean and have my breakfast.

Calling Mum wasn't the best decision—but when do I ever make good decisions? Present Lucy is stranded in the middle of the Great Ocean Road with her best friend. I mean, that's half a good decision, at least.

'Oi Lucy, what the hell are you doing out there?'

Because I'm in good company.

'Avoiding your stinky arse!' I toss the apple core into the trees below and jump onto the road. 'You didn't stop farting *allllll* night.'

'Yeah, yeah, whatever.' She lights a cigarette and leans on the side of the car. Her silver hair is tied into a top bun, and her eyeliner has smudged under her hazel eyes. She shuts her eyes and takes a deep drag. She's exhausted—from what, I can't say.

'Help me with this tyre,' she says after a few minutes, stubbing out her cigarette on the cracked bitumen.

She places one of the blankets beneath us, finds the jack, positions it under the car and we both push our weight into it to lift it. Cars are goddamn heavy.

'What did your mum want?' It's sometimes uncanny how well Liz knows what's going on.

'Just wanted to know where I am. She's not mad, though.'

She gives me an incredulous look, yanking the rim off her deflated tyre. 'Seriously? I figured she'd be spewing.'

I shrug, taking the rim from her before she can throw it into the ocean. 'She wants to talk about things when I get back.'

'Like what?' Liz grunts as she starts to unscrew the nuts from the wheel.

I hesitate. 'Uni and stuff.'

'Why?'

We're both sweating. The wheel pops off and Liz rolls it to the side. For a second, I hope she's too busy with the whole changing-the-tyre business to realise I'm having heart palpitations at the thought of telling her.

She finds the spare in the boot and pins me with a look that says, 'You're not getting out of this.' Shit.

'I just—it's hard to explain,' I mumble, reaching for the screws to help her place them on the spare.

'Try.'

'I—' I pause, staring at the broken bitumen beneath me. Why is it so hard? 'I'm not going back to uni.'

Liz stops twisting, a nut half screwed into the tyre. We're beside each other, arms touching, faces damp, my heart in my throat. When I lift my head, Liz's gaze is soft.

'Why didn't you say anything?' She drops the wrench and motions for me to sit down against the rock face behind us. I follow. The asphalt digs into the backs of my thighs, the jagged edges of the rock finding the soft places along my spine.

Because you're so much better than me. I fell asleep in all my classes. I couldn't focus on lectures. I dropped subjects and couldn't hand in assessments on time.

'It's not that big a deal.'

'It is, Luce.' Liz grabs my hand. 'I know how much it sucked for you.' She sighs, a long weary one that has me flicking my eyes to her. She's looking at our hands, her brown skin against my olive. My nails are chewed, hers are manicured a pastel blue.

'Does this mean you're gonna do graphic design?' There's a spark of something in her voice. Hope? My stomach plummets at the thought of going back to study.

'No.' I pull my hand from her grip and cross my arms over

my chest. 'I wouldn't be that good at it.'

As stubborn as ever, Liz grabs my arm and pulls me into an awkward one-sided hug. 'Shut the hell up, Lien Tran. You'd be an amazing graphic designer.'

'I make your YouTube thumbnails 'cause you're useless with Photoshop. It's just a hobby.'

'Then what do you call your comic? Daydreaming? It's *talent*. I know it when I see it. I've been telling you for *years*.'

I shrink away from her words, her confidence in me. It's not true. Hurt passes over her face, so vulnerable for a split second before she's back to Liz. Soft and firm and as weightless as air. You could breathe her in and feel like you're on top of the world.

But all I feel right now is nothing.

'I tried to tell them about it, you know. They just… didn't get it.'

'What did they say?'

I do the best impression of Dad I can, all stern and confused and dumbfounded that his only daughter wants to die most days of the week. '*Lien, you're making this up. Why are you sad? You have nothing to be sad for.*'

We're quiet for a longer moment, arms loosely wrapped around each other.

'You didn't bring anything with you, did you?'

'I've been clean for three weeks.'

'And I leave in a month,' she whispers so softly it catches in the breeze.

The sun moves from behind the clouds, bathing us in a gentle touch of warmth. The space around us sighs just as I do.

'I don't want to leave if you're like this,' Liz says.

The words flood to my throat: *then don't*. But they don't break through. I smile and intertwine our fingers. 'You've been dreaming of New York since you were ten, Liz.'

'You should come with me. Name a more iconic duo, I'll wait.'

It's such a crazy suggestion, I choke out a laugh. 'With what money?'

'I can pay for some of it.' She's smiling at me now, her classic toothy grin that always makes me grin right back. I can feel my lips tugging upwards despite how goddamn shit I'm feeling. 'It'll be an adventure!'

'You already paid for *this* trip.' I kick myself every time I think about how useless I am. No job, no prospects, no anything.

'You could just come with me. You could even *audition* with me.' She nudges my arm.

'You know I have stage fright. I'm not cut out for theatre.'

'Don't let your dreams be dreams.'

'But they *are* dreams,' I reply. 'I want to be that girl who rocks up and magically lands her dream job, finds a down-to-earth boy who thinks I'm the world, and I live with our two cats in a cute apartment while struggling to pay rent.'

Liz sighs, shaking her head at me with a small smile.

The weight of dread in my body is dissolving like a bath bomb. Liz is now talking about what songs she should sing for her auditions ('I could totally rap "Guns and Ships", make Daveed Diggs proud.') and what dance routine would be the one that shows off her best '*assets*'. We finish replacing the tyre while singing the opening song to *The Greatest Showman*. Our hands are streaked with grease and dirt, our shirts clinging to our backs, but I haven't felt this happy in a long time. It hits me hard in the chest: this is how I am when I'm with Liz.

Happy.

But I know this will end, this moment of shared contentment. Because I can't go with her. Not this time.

We're good to get back on the road just after midday. We wash our hands with bottled water, and eat bruised apples and salted chips as Liz drives. The slopes of lush mountains crest the right side of us. The sun is high, warm on the tops of my bare thighs. Sitting here in our silence feels like it did at the beginning of the trip, smooth and carefree, like the last days of high school when all we did was drink, watch shows and sleep in the same bed. We play 'I Spy', scream the lyrics to the first act of the *Hamilton* soundtrack, and I sketch until we arrive at our destination: Loch Ard Gorge.

This place is definitely Instagram-worthy. Two rock formations have created a small alcove along the shore. The tips of the formations don't meet; the horizon is just beyond, like a calling for me to get out of the damn car and go swimming.

And there's nobody around. It's like we've been blessed by the social media gods.

We snap our photos, apply appropriate filters, then we're naked and in the water. It's heavenly; warm enough to feel soft, like satin on our skin. Sea foam clings to our hair and maybe in another life we were mermaids. Liz's GoPro is out and she's hiding most of her body from the camera, but the hint of her bare shoulders is a clear indicator to her subs that she's definitely not wearing a bikini.

'Hi, fam! We're at Loch Ard Gorge and *look at this view*!' She does a pano with the camera and I duck as it passes me. When she's done, we play 'Marco Polo', look for shells under the mounds of sand, and laugh so much my stomach starts to cramp. It feels so good to laugh with Liz, like champagne bubbles in my chest. I don't know how long we're there for, but eventually the sun turns the clouds purple and pink. The sea is chilling and we run out to dry off, put some clothes on our bodies, and sit on the sand to watch the sunset. I never see things like this at home, these natural wonders that happen every day. I'm usually twisted on my chair in front of my Wacom sketching or watching the smoke from nearby industrials fog up the sky. This air around us is clean and salted and tastes like freedom. We eat half-melted Red Skins and pass a bottle of ginger ale between us. This is how it should be between us always; I never want to be a step behind her. This is where I'm safe, where I'm home.

'What are you thinking, Luce?'

I sigh, drinking the last of the ginger ale and frowning at the horizon. 'That I want to stay here with you forever.'

Liz chuckles and reaches for another Red Skin. 'I know. This is pretty awesome.' She rips a chunk of red and slowly starts to chew the lolly. 'So when are Kelsey and Jane getting updated?'

'When I get home. I told everyone I was on a semi-hiatus. They'll understand if it's late.'

'Your art style has really improved, though. I'm loving it right now.'

'So have your dance moves.'

Liz playfully smacks my arm. 'Those moves got me to New York.'

'You mean your *one* viral dance routine to Camila's "Havana" got you to New York.'

After our shared laughter comes a silence broken only by the crashing of waves and birds flying above us. The sun slides past the rock formations, the tips of the structures bathed in amber. I imagine standing on the edge of the rock, the water roaring below and the horizon under my fingertips. It's terrifying, to be so high and unsure. What awaits me in the water?

I don't want to know. Instead, I take the leap.

'I think I'll look up some graphic design courses when I get home,' I tell Liz. She's the only one I want to tell, the only one who understands. 'I know Billy Blue offers some, and I saw an online one recently.'

Her response is what I expect: a lot of squealing, hugging and words of encouragement. 'You got this.' She's determined to keep me on this course. 'I believe in you.'

'I won't do it right away. I need time.'

'I know.'

The fading light catches the beads of water on her face, like tiny crystals embedded in her skin. For a moment, everything feels smaller, warmer and firmer under the glow of the sun. Here we are, sitting side-by-side once again, and I want nothing more than to stay here. I want this moment to swallow me whole. And when she smiles at me, it splits her face open like the sun breaking the dawn.

'What?'

'You're going to be okay, Lucy,' she grabs my hand and threads our fingers together. 'We're going to be okay.'

And for once, I believe her.

Afterdeath

BY

CASSI DORIAN

When I wake up, I realise with absolute certainty that I am dead.

I feel nothing

nothing

nothing

not inside and not

around me.

It is a strange feeling. If I touch something, say the floor, it's as if it's not quite real. I can touch it but it does not exist, not anymore, not for me. I can feel it but it is not there. Or I am not there.

I look down at my watch and notice it's stopped working. The second hand moves irregularly, jumping forwards and backwards by odd increments. The face is smashed. I shake my hand, and shattered glass drops to the floor. My skin is covered in small abrasions.

Perhaps I am some sort of ghost. I stand and look in the mirror. I am surprised that I can see myself in the mirror at all, but I suppose I am not a vampire, as they are *undead*. I am *definitely* dead. The side of my skull is somewhat crushed. My dark brown hair is matted and blood-soaked. I am very, very pale. Faint veins are visible through my skin. I am hollow.

I never meant to kill myself, it just happened… I think. Or I didn't think. I am quite sure it was an accident though. I was despairing. I was out of my mind. Romy, my Romy, was lying on the floor. I can see him now, still lying there. Lying there and not breathing at all. Not now and not then.

As if possessed, I reach up to pat the bloody side of my head. I can faintly recall being weightless. I sway at the thought. I imagine my skull colliding with the corner of the table, slicing through until my brain tissue leaks out all over the floor and blood pools around my head.

Looking at myself in the mirror, I see that my brain is not exposed at all. Instead I see a section of my skull; there is a tiny spot of white bone amongst the black, sticky blood. I want to touch it and poke my finger through the gaping flesh and dig my way into the soft and squishy brain tissue.

I walk over to Romy, who is lying on the floor, and kneel beside him. I kiss his forehead, his cheeks, his dead lips. I am repulsed. I nestle myself in the crook of his armpit so it is like he is comforting me. I am also dead, I remember.

A spider crawls on his arm. Its black body is the size of my thumbnail and it has short legs.

'Go away,' I tell it.

Another joins and, together, they begin to walk across his chest. I shoo them. More spiders start crawling over his corpse. They cross his legs, his arms, his neck. Soon there are a dozen, then two.

I untangle myself from his body. I try to brush them off, flinching as their fragile legs scuttle over my fingers.

'Leave him alone,' I say. I grow frustrated. 'Leave him *alone*.' I blink rapidly to push back the tears. I use the base of my palms to dig into my eyes until the darkness forms strange patterns on my eyelids. If I pay more attention, I realise they are the patterns in the rug. An inhuman sound escapes my mouth.

It takes my eyes a moment to adjust and clear the patterns from my vision. Romy is no longer lying on the floor. He is sitting on the red velvet chair in my lounge room, staring at me. I want to scream but I'm scared spiders will crawl out of my mouth, because they've all disappeared, and my stomach is churning.

My head begins to throb. Pain explodes in my skull. I look at Romy in fear.

'What's happening?' I ask. I fall to my knees, doubled over. My face is scrunched tight, my teeth are clenched. Hands grasp my wrists and pull them from my face. They're gentle hands, have always been gentle hands, but they're still not quite real. It's not the same. They're ghost hands. I'm pulled into him.

'Are you here?' I squeeze the words out through gritted teeth.

'I'm right next to you, Hülya,' he says.

'You weren't breathing,' I say. 'That's all I remember.'

He pulls me closer, leaning his forehead against mine. He doesn't seem to mind the gaping hole in my head. 'I'm sorry,' he says, over and over and over and over. 'I'm sorry, I'm sorry,

I'm sorry.' It becomes like an echo. I hear it all around me and I hear it outside this room, outside my mind. I don't know what he's sorry *for*.

I sit there for what could be all of eternity, or only a few minutes, hearing the words on repeat. Time is finite, time is endless. I am nowhere.

'Romy.' He stops talking and opens his eyes. They are magic, those eyes—a crystal blue, an open sky. I lose myself for a moment. I forget it all.

'Where do you think we are?' he asks.

'I don't know… Barzakh? Purgatory? Siberia?'

'Siberia?'

'A place of exile. Don't you think?'

'I don't know,' he replies. 'This is your death.'

'It's yours too!' I release myself from his embrace and analyse my surroundings. The high ceilings, the familiar prints on the wall, the cabinet of expensive china that nobody can use, the mismatched furniture.

'It's a shame this is the first time I've ever been to your house,' he says.

I can't help but laugh. 'Circumstances could've been better.'

He smiles back at me. He is still wearing his school uniform—a navy jumper and grey pants. His shoes are off. He is beautiful even now. I walk over to the door and try the knob.

'It won't open.' I wrench the handle and push my weight against the door. 'I don't understand. It doesn't even have a lock; how can it not open?' I slam my body against it repeatedly but I feel nothing, and it still doesn't give. It's like an invisible force is pushing back. I run over to the window and try to pull it open. It doesn't budge. I let out a growl as I exert a final show of force.

'Aren't you going to help?' I yell at Romy. I turn and see him standing alone in the centre of the room, impassive. A bruise starts blossoming over his left eye. There is a galaxy spreading under his skin. Gaseous clouds of navy and purple and yellow forming a stellar nursery more delicate than any in the universe. I forget about the door and the window. I run to him.

'Who hurt you?' I ask him gently.

'You don't know?'

'I don't remember anything.'

'Well, what was the last thing you remember?'

'Walking into the room and you were dead on the floor.'

'What about before that?'

Nothing. There are gaps, I can see them, these empty black patches in my memory.

'We were at school,' I say. 'Sitting in the library, in our corner.'

'What else?'

I search my mind. I go deeper. I try to swim in the holes, but I can only dip my feet in.

'You kissed me.' I smile, I remember that. 'At school. You said you couldn't help it. We never did that before.'

'That's right.'

'But there's more.'

'A bit more,' he says, 'but let's not worry about it right now.' He sits down on the rug and I lay my head in his lap, facing up towards the ceiling. I close my eyes while he brushes my hair behind my ears. He hums a song.

We are in his room. Music plays quietly in the background. I open my eyes and he bends down to kiss me. Everything smells like him and I'm home.

'How long can you stay?' he asks.

'A little while. My parents think I'm studying at the library for the Bio exam.'

'Should you be studying for the exam? I don't want to be a distraction.'

'Please, I spend every other waking moment of my life studying, I deserve a break.'

I'd be happy if I never had to pick up another textbook again. I hate that I'm good at everything my parents want me to be good at—everything that would get me into the right university degree.

'I wish you never had to go,' Romy says.

'Me too. I feel like this is the one place I can actually be myself.' I lift my hands up and intertwine them around his neck. I'm not usually so corny but I mean it. I'm tired of the rules I'm supposed to know, and the ways I'm supposed to act. I'm tired of working so hard in school but having my future decided for me. I'm tired of the pressure. Lately, the thing I'm tired of the most is pretending I barely know Romy when I know everything about him.

I know he dreams of being an environmental scientist, not a lawyer, that he listens to the song 'Julia' by The Beatles on repeat before he goes to sleep and doesn't know why, that he sees a psychologist once a week because he says he's empty inside, that his favourite colour is forest green, and that if I blow a raspberry on him it never fails to make him laugh.

'I love…' I pause. I want to say it, because I mean it, and I'm not sure why I can't. The words hang between us. He knows I love him, he must. '…spending time with you.'

He lifts my head from his lap and lies down next to me. I kiss him with all my unsaid feelings and he puts his hands on my waist and brings me into him. I am trapped in a bear hug, my body enveloped by his long arms and legs, my head lost somewhere in the soft folds of his jumper. His arms are tight around me and everything is dark and warm. I am in a cave made completely out of Romy.

'Same,' he says.

I smile into his hoodie. I can feel him smiling too. I lie there for what seems like an eternity.

'We're lucky your parents are never home.' The words come out muffled and barely recognisable.

'What's that?' he jokes. 'You want to play chess?'

When I open my eyes again I'm in the lounge, still lying on Romy's lap. His fingertips are gentle on my scalp and on my shoulder and on my chest, making faint patterns on my body. His ghost fingers glide underneath my clothes and through my hair. I can almost pretend it's real.

'Romy, did someone find out about us?'

He traces the letters *Y E S* onto my skin. The letters burn me. I recall the sickening fear, the feeling of dread, the heavy weight in the pit of my stomach that comes when a secret is no longer a secret, when your one sanctuary has been discovered by people who wish it never existed.

I crawl away and dry retch, but the dread is too heavy for me to expel. It just sits there in the depths of my stomach, slowly chewing its way through the lining so it can enter my bloodstream. I can feel it bubbling within me. I want it out.

My stomach heaves. Black sludge dribbles from my mouth. It's thick and vile.

It's made from shame.

I crawl over to the potted plant by the window and empty my guts into the soil. Toxic fumes evaporate from the gunk, and the leaves curl over and die.

'I feel much better now,' I mumble. I am released. I am lighter than air. 'Are my teeth black?' I flash Romy a big smile.

'That was really disgusting.' He hands me a tissue. 'You look like death.'

'Hilarious.' I wipe my face clean, dispose of the tissue and pull him up from the rug. He places one of his hands on my waist and clasps the other around my own bruised one. I lead him into a slow dance. I make him spin me in circles and dip me, so that my spine arches towards the floor and my hair hangs almost to the ground. He hums his song.

There's something else to it though, to the song. In the background, a very faint, very rhythmic, beeping.

'Do you hear that?' I ask.

'Hear what?'

'That noise.'

It's weak and I can't tell where it's coming from.

'I don't hear a noise.'

I stop the dancing and listen more closely. It's all around me, getting louder. There is no source.

Beep   beep   beep

Constant.

I cover my ears but it's *inside* my head. Every six beats—*beep*.

Romy looks at me strangely.

'What do you mean you can't hear it?' I say. 'It won't stop.'

Beep   beep   beep

'*Ugh*, this is torture!' I go and try the door again. He wanders around with a confused look on his face, searching for a sound he can't hear. I shake the handle. I need to leave this place. I've had enough now. I take a few steps back and hurl myself at the door with all my strength.

Still nothing.

I feel nothing.

Nothing feels *real*.

Nothing except for the bruises that are just blooming on the crease of my elbow. The skin is tender there, and if I touch the right place there is a sharp sting. My head is clouded by this maddening beeping noise and the pain from my head wound and the soreness from the bruises all over my body. All at once they consume my senses and disorientate me. I feel like these things keep happening *to* me but not *because* of me. It's infuriating.

'Let me out!' I have no control, I realise. I have no way to move on.

To move on?

I turn to Romy, who is looking more tired by the minute. At this moment I know he's not here with me. That this is not his death, and that his happened in a different way, in a different time and space. He's here because of me, but he isn't being kept here like I am.

'Romy, what if… what if I'm stuck here? What if this place is my hell?' The thought is terrifying. I see my afterlife stretching out before me in its infinity—an eternal nonexistence awaits. *Death isn't fair*, I muse bitterly.

'You're not trapped, Jewel,' he says. My chest spasms at the mention of his name for me. 'I'm trying to get you to remember.'

'Well it's hard when all I can hear is this freaking beeping noise in my head!' I know it's wrong to take it out on him, and I immediately want to take it back.

'Just close your eyes for a minute,' he says, and I do.

'I feel so guilty,' says Romy. It's his turn, and he moves one of his pawns to protect his queen. We're sitting on his bed with the chess board lying crookedly between us.

'I feel so alive!' I say it overdramatically but it's true—I don't feel bad at all. I'm used to it now, the lying to my parents and sneaking over to Romy's place. It's the only way we can be alone together—without judgement and without fear. I move my castle out, ready to attack.

'I mean, I wouldn't change anything, I just wish we didn't have to be so secretive.'

'We wouldn't have to be if you were a Turkish boy,' I tease him. I smile as I say it but I feel so sad inside because I know it's true. Anne and baba would love Romy if they gave him a chance. He is polite and clever and never refuses food. But I know them. They would be... disappointed if I brought him to dinner, and I know it would be the same with Romy's parents.

'Or if you weren't a Muslim girl.'

'That too.' It's something we both understand. Just one of those things. An offhand comment, a subtle suggestion, never outwardly dissuaded. Everything is okay as long as it's not your child. It's not fair. I know it would be fine eventually, after time. But we're not quite there yet. I want to make sure it's worth the trouble.

Romy moves his bishop and takes out my castle.

'I should have seen that coming!' I take a moment to think a few moves ahead. He's made his king vulnerable without realising. We move pieces back and forth across the board and I attempt to set a trap. Most of the pieces have been taken. He still has a few powerful players: his queen, both castles, and some pawns. I've lost both my castles now, and my queen, but I've got my knights and my bishops and a couple of pawns to see me through.

We're silent for a while. It takes longer and longer to make each decision. I move my knight into prime king-killing position. He doesn't see it coming.

'Checkmate.' I take his most valuable piece.

He gives me a mischievous grin.

~

'That's how you got your black eye,' I say to Romy, 'you got into a fight.'

'I didn't mean to.' He curls over like he's just been punched in the stomach, and stumbles backwards a little. He's been winded and he gasps for breath. The sound is raspy and pitiful.

'It was my brother,' I realise.

I remember.

Selim saw us in the library that day, during last period. We didn't know at the time. I let Romy walk me part-way home from school after class. We only live one street over from each other, but usually I walk with my brother or by myself. He was insistent. He said he wasn't feeling good but couldn't explain why. 'I just want to be near you,' he said.

About halfway I heard a shout behind me. It was Selim. Romy let go of my hand without drawing attention to it. I wasn't too worried. I could explain Romy walking me home for just today.

'I saw you,' he said. Selim closed the gap between us so quickly it scared me. It took a moment to figure out what was going on. I stepped forward to ask what he meant but he interrupted me. He took Romy by the jumper. 'I saw you with my sister.' Selim's eyes were vicious. Romy put his hands up.

'I care about her,' he said.

'You were taking advantage of her,' Selim replied.

'You're being ridicious,' I said, 'I can take care of myself.'

'Shut up, Hülya,' Selim said. 'You don't know what you're

talking about.' He pushed Romy back and advanced again.

'Just stop it,' I said, 'please.' Selim had anger issues. It might be because things always came slowly for him. He would get upset—overreact, get emotional, always be quick to judge. But he was loyal and caring, too. He was just overprotective.

'You stay away from her.'

'She can make up her own mind.'

'She doesn't know what you boys are like.' Push, push, push. Voices raised. Romy with his hands in the air.

'Well she knows me better than you think.' It sounded worse than he meant it. Selim shoved Romy to the ground.

The memory fades, and I notice that bits of wallpaper are starting to flake from the walls around us.

'I'm sorry,' I tell Romy, 'about my brother.' Blood starts pouring out of his nose while he's crouched on the ground protecting his stomach. He groans a little.

'Not… your… fault.' He takes a sharp breath between each word. His right hand is covered in dried blood. He unclenches his fist and shakes it.

It's raining little sheets of pearly grey above us. They float from the walls into my hair and onto my clothes. They're slightly damp.

'You broke his nose.'

'It was… an accident.'

'None of it should have happened.' I'm so angry.

'I know.'

'Run,' I had said to Romy. 'I'll take care of this.' He looked wrecked, standing strangely, breathing cautiously. Selim was clutching his face, which was caked with blood. It was hard to tell who looked worse after it all. Romy looked worried but left.

Now, there is blood dripping from his nose to the floor. I take his mottled fist gently in my hands.

'Lift your head to the sky,' I tell him.

Romy looks up. 'Is it snowing?'

'Jewel, I feel like I'm broken.'

The chess board lies on the ground, the pieces scattered and fallen. He says the words so quietly, as if he is scared for them to exist in the open. I am curled up like a cat. I twist my head so I can see his face. He looks asleep and, for a moment, I think I have imagined it.

'What do you mean?' We are the only people in the house but I whisper the words.

'I don't know how to explain it…' He pauses. He's silent for so long I think he may have fallen asleep. 'Right now, for example. This is perfect, just me and you. This is where I want to be. But I'm so unhappy, Jewel. I don't know if unhappy is the right word. Something is missing. It's like there's this weight on my brain and I can't think properly.'

I hear his voice break when he says the word 'unhappy'. I see the pills on his bedside table. I see his brows creased from trying to find the right way to say this.

'I don't feel… right,' he says. He's looking at me like he wants me to understand. His expression is so vulnerable that it worries me.

'I want to help.' I pull him closer. At the moment it's all I can do.

'You do help.'

~

The day I died, Romy was in my house. My parents had taken Selim to the emergency room after his fight with Romy. I was home alone and he just showed up on my doorstep. He looked dreadful. His words were unintelligible. He was a mess. He stumbled into the house and I sat him on the couch in the lounge. I told him to wait a moment while I got my phone so we could call someone. I couldn't remember where I'd put it. When I finally found it and came back, he wasn't breathing.

I look at Romy now and see him staring at me. 'How is your nose now?' I ask.

'I think it's stopped bleeding,' he says.

The wallpaper around us peels off in bigger and bigger chunks. Most glide through the air like paper aeroplanes, drifting around the room until they cover the ground, but some merely drop, too soaked with water to float down. Above, the ceiling is heavy. I haven't got long until it falls through.

I get up and trace the outline of the half-fallen wallpaper. The plasterboard behind it is glistening wet. The walls are crying. Droplets run down from the ceiling.

Romy pulls me to the couch and we sit down, knees pulled up and touching.

'I know what you're thinking,' he says.

'And what's that?'

'I didn't try to kill myself.'

'You overdosed.'

'I did.'

'But why?'

He shifts uneasily. I can tell he's ashamed. He casts his gaze downwards and inhales deeply.

'I was really down that day, even before the fight. Then that happened and I panicked. I thought I was going to lose you and I was just so overwhelmed. I wasn't thinking clearly and I was in so much pain. I broke down. There was no one home. I was so sick of being alone. I just wanted to calm down a bit. I took the rest of my pills and some of Mum's pain medication. I didn't realise how strong it was. After I did it I freaked out, and for some reason I thought you'd know what to do.' He laughs humourlessly. 'I know it doesn't make sense now, but I guess it did at the time.'

Knowing that all this was an accident almost kills me again. I can't bear the way Romy looks at me now. I can see he's in pain and it hurts me because it's all too late. So instead I look around. It's raining harder than ever. The room has begun to flood. Water flows between my toes. I smell antiseptic and disinfectant. It's the smell of a hospital. The ceiling cracks open and water gushes into the lounge. The room begins to fill.

I realise I can feel things again. Not just weird localised feelings of pain, but everything and everywhere. It's so cold. I've got goosebumps and I'm shivering all over. The world around me is seeping into my pores.

I'm not sure if I'm a ghost any longer.

'Why haven't you asked me what happened to my head?'

'I already know,' Romy says.

'But how? It happened after you died.' I have to shout to be heard over the rushing of the water. I remember now. I was distraught when I found him. I screamed. Angry tears rolled down my cheeks and my life was ruined. He was *gone*. I loved him and he was gone, forever and ever, and he was not coming back. That was all I could feel and nothing else but the burning anger in my throat.

I smashed my fists on the hardwood floor and called an ambulance. I punched a wall hard, swivelled on my heels and flung myself onto his body, which was warm, I think. Still warm. I sobbed and screamed his name and didn't want to wait for the fucking ambulance because my life was over.

Then I got up too fast.

I felt dizzy.

I was dehydrated.

I had cried all the water out of my body and it was now a salty mess drying on my cheeks and on my neck. We were in my lounge room.

On the floor was the rug that my family brought back from Istanbul, on our last visit to see my dede and anneanne in Turkey. It was an antique *hah*, handspun by young women in a mountain village of Anatolia. We bought it from a rug dealer who was a friend of the family. He talked for what seemed like hours about the symbolism of the woven images. I forget almost all of what he said, except about how some patterns repeat themselves infinitely.

I stepped back and tripped on the rug.

I fell
and fell
and fell
quickly and endlessly.
And then nothing.

Most of the ceiling has caved in, and it's like a waterfall is pouring through the roof. The water has reached my waist. We're going to drown.

I wade through the flotsam. I've lost him.

Beep   beep   beep

Rushing water. Antiseptic. Raining inside.

Bruises in the creases of my elbows.

Water creeping up my body.

My head in pain.

Swimming.

Time is water.

'Jewel, can you hear me?' A gentle voice. *His* voice.

'Where are you?' My arms and legs work tirelessly to keep me afloat. Furniture knocks into me. I frantically look around.

'I'm here.'

I let myself sink.

'Jewel, I'm right next to you.'

And when I wake up, he is.

Living Rose

BY

KANEANA MAY

Olive's fingers speed over the keys on her phone. She presses *Share* on her 'Saturday arvo study sesh' post. An image of her textbooks, notepad, pens and green tea is posted online.

Rose comes into the kitchen and peers over Olive's shoulder to see what she's doing. 'Let me guess,' Rose muses, 'Eat, Sleep, Study, Repeat?'

Damn it. Olive likes that caption better and contemplates editing her post.

'Tell Mum and Dad I've gone to the movies,' Rose says, grabbing the car keys.

'I thought you were going to finish your essay?'

Rose shrugs. 'It can wait.'

Can it? Olive knows it's due Monday. And when Rose told their parents earlier that she was going to *finish* her English essay, Olive knew she meant *start* her essay.

'You've got a problem with me going out?' Rose's eyes are wide, her eyebrows arching, as she reads Olive's response.

'Well, you didn't even ask me if I needed the car,' Olive points out.

'*Do* you need it?'

No. But that isn't really the point.

'Do you want to come to the movies with us?' Rose offers. 'I'm going with Ella.'

Olive doesn't mind Ella, especially compared to some of Rose's other friends, but Olive can't just *go to the movies*. All week she's planned on spending Saturday afternoon studying. In fact, she spends every Saturday afternoon studying. She can't just throw that plan out the window to go see a movie. 'I've got study to do.'

'Suit yourself,' Rose shrugs, not bothered either way.

Olive fights the feeling of annoyance building in her stomach as Rose turns from the door with some parting words: 'You're only a teenager for seven years of your life, you've got decades to be an adult.'

Olive's mouth tightens as she listens to Rose's footsteps heading out to the car. She lets herself wonder for just a second if Rose is right, but quickly pushes the thought away. All *this* that she's doing is part of a lifelong plan.

Rose just doesn't get that.

Olive arrives home after her morning job at the newsagency, followed by an afternoon volunteering at the local nursing home. Her feet are aching from standing up all day and she's tired but has hours of study ahead of her.

She moves into the lounge room where Rose is propped against the couch. Magazines are sprawled across the floor, scissors in hand as she cuts out pictures. It reminds Olive of art projects they had to do years ago, in early high school.

'What are you doing?'

'Making a pin board of all the places I want to travel to.' She chucks her mobile at Olive. 'Take a photo of me. Make sure you get all the mags in.'

Olive sighs but takes a photo and hands the phone back. 'What are you going to caption it? "How to make your lounge room look like a disaster zone"?'

Rose laughs, choosing to be amused, rather than offended. She quickly clicks at her phone, uploading the photo straight away. As she types, she tells Olive, 'Future plans! Hashtag WorldHereICome.'

Olive feels her body tensing as it often does at Rose's carefree attitude. She spies a picture of the Eiffel Tower and can't help but shake her head. 'How are you going to afford to get to Paris? You borrowed money off me last week for petrol to get into town.'

But Rose isn't fazed. 'You gotta dream, sis.'

Olive studies her little sister's face. There's an innocence and naivety about Rose that always makes Olive feel much more than thirteen months older. Logical thoughts don't seem to enter Rose's head, just wistful ones. Olive wishes she didn't continuously have to bring her back down to earth. 'You're still going to need money.'

Rose shrugs. 'I'll figure it out.'

Olive doesn't know why she lets Rose's laissez-faire attitude bother her so much. Olive's always planning and thinking three steps ahead, whereas her sister only ever lives in the moment.

Olive feels like she's waiting for it all to catch up with Rose, and then she can have her moment of victory.

'Don't you want to travel?' Rose peers up at her as she cuts around the Statue of Liberty.

Of course she does, but after school she'll be going to uni. 'One day,' Olive shrugs as she realises Rose has pretty much cut out pictures of all the major landmarks around the world. 'Maybe you should stick to places in Australia? Might be a bit more realistic?'

But Rose, happily cutting, doesn't even look up.

Olive casts her eyes over the sprawl of pictures, magazines and abandoned scrap paper. Her skin prickles with irritation. 'It'd be easier to do this on Pinterest.'

Rose looks up now. 'You mean neater?' She smiles, well aware Olive can't handle mess. 'But this way is more fun.'

Olive forces herself to take a breath. 'How long have you been doing this?'

'I dunno, what's the time?'

'Almost five.'

Rose is amused. 'I started after breakfast.'

'You've been doing this *all* day?'

'All day,' Rose confirms.

Olive doesn't know whether to feel jealous or sorry for her sister. Rose has wasted a whole day mindlessly dreaming of faraway places from their lounge room floor.

~

'I've been thinking about what you said.'

Olive looks up from pouring a green smoothie into a bowl. She says a lot of things, so who knows what Rose is talking about. 'What's that?'

'About travelling around Australia instead of the world.'

Olive grabs the homemade muesli she managed to make late last night and sprinkles it over the smoothie.

'Did you know there's a "Dog on the Tuckerbox"?'

'A what?' Olive can feel her face all scrunched up as she places two extra green apples, a stick of celery and some spinach on the chopping board.

'A statue of a dog on a tuckerbox,' Rose says. 'It's at a place called Snake Gully. It's near Gundagai… I wonder if Mum and Dad have been there?' Rose produces her phone to show Olive a picture she found online.

'And you want to see it?' Olive pushes herself up on top of a stool, so she has a bird's-eye view of her green smoothie bowl and extra greens.

'Yeah,' Rose smiles wide, 'it's cool.'

'Is it?' Olive pulls her phone from her pocket and takes a photo.

Rose shakes her head. 'You don't get it.'

'No, I don't.'

'There's a whole story about it on here. It's in honour of the pioneers. You'd appreciate it—you like history and all that stuff.' Rose reaches out and moves Olive's spoon farther away from the bowl and reangles the celery.

Olive nods at Rose, acknowledging it looks better, and takes another photo. She uploads it straight away with the caption 'Start the day right. Green smoothie bowl love.'

'Anyway,' Rose says, 'I'm going to travel around the country and check out all the weird things in Australia.'

'Rose's Weird and Wacky Aussie Tour,' Olive jokes.

'Yes! That's what I'm calling it,' Rose exclaims as she picks up Olive's spoon. 'You're a genius,' she adds, scooping a mouthful of Olive's smoothie bowl. Olive thinks about shooing her hand away, but instead just sighs; she knows by now that Rose will help herself anyway.

'I had the best afternoon,' Rose announces as she collapses into her chair at the dinner table.

Olive watches her younger sister as she slides into her own chair. Her head hurts after a full day at school and an afternoon of study. She still hasn't checked everything off her to-do list, so she will be back at her desk after dinner.

'What'd you do, love?' their dad asks, his head down, focused on his Tuesday-night tacos—his favourite, second only to their weekly Sunday roast.

Rose shrugs, pushing her hair off her face. 'Me and Ella just hung out at the beach.'

'Ella and I,' Olive corrects as she assembles her taco.

Rose rolls her eyes. '*Ella and I* sunbaked and went for a swim.'

'And had the "world's best ice cream",' Olive quotes from

Rose's Instagram post, which she tagged '#getinmybelly'. It already had seventy-two likes, compared to Olive's smoothie bowl from yesterday, which only has thirteen. Olive found herself fighting the familiar feelings of not being good enough, pretty enough, popular enough, when she noticed it earlier. Insecurity always haunts her when she compares her popularity to her sister's. Sometimes Olive wonders why she bothers posting at all.

'It was so good!' Rose's face fills with happiness just thinking about the ice cream.

'Sounds like a lovely afternoon,' their mother comments.

'The *best*,' Olive reminds them.

Rose knows Olive is having a dig. 'You should try it sometime.'

But Olive doesn't get it. She never gets it. For Olive, a 'best day' is when she tops an exam or when her report card comes home. 'Did you do any study for your exams?' Olive can't help herself.

Rose jerks her head up and meets Olive's gaze. Her bright sunshiny eyes have quickly turned stormy. 'Really?' Irritation tugs at her face.

'When are your exams, Rose?' their father asks, suddenly looking up. Their parents have never had to hassle Olive about studying or assignments, and they often seem to forget that Rose is more about everything else than she is about school work.

Rose shoots Olive a look, her mouth twisting, probably

debating whether or not to tell the truth.

The words are dancing around in Olive's mouth, desperate to escape, but she forcibly bites down on her lip, knowing it'll cause a fight if she says any more.

'Rose?' their mum's tone has tensed. 'When are they?'

'My first one is on Wednesday,' she says finally.

'As in tomorrow?' their mum clarifies.

Rose exhales loudly, confirming this is the case.

Their parents exchange a familiar look of frustration.

'Olive, the dishes are yours tonight. It sounds like Rose has some study to do.'

A stream of arguments come battling to the forefront of her mind. It's Rose's turn. She has her own study to do. Why should she be punished because Rose once again has neglected her school work? But instead of saying anything, she just sighs. Fighting won't make a difference.

She casts her eyes back over to Rose, who, despite being annoyed about her own impending study, smirks that Olive's been lumped with the dishes.

'Hurry up, Rose! I need the bathroom!' As Olive waits in the hallway she uploads a photo she took of her yoga mat and the early morning light. 'Yoga Zen Wednesday'. She didn't actually get the chance to do yoga this morning, but nobody needs to know that, right? She knocks again. 'Rose?!'

'All right, all right.' Rose flings the door open. She's still in her pyjamas and her hair is in a messy bun on top of her head.

'What have you been doing? You're not even ready for school.' Olive's exasperated; she's been waiting to get into the bathroom for the last twenty minutes.

'My makeup's done,' she says a little proudly, but quickly dismisses Olive's annoyance. 'Did you know there's a place in South Australia called the Blue Lake? And it changes colour at different times of the year?'

Olive shakes her head as she grabs her brush and starts running it through her hair. 'No, I didn't know that.'

'And did you know that there's a place in the Northern Territory that's known as the UFO capital of Australia?'

Olive's confused. 'Are these facts for your exams?'

'No!' Rose laughs, amused by the thought. 'I did some more research for my Weird and Wacky Tour.'

Olive feels like screaming. This time last year, Olive had spent months studying for her Year Eleven exams, but Rose, on the morning of her own exams, is reciting facts for a dream holiday. How are they even related? 'If you want a lift with me, I'm leaving in twenty. Otherwise you'll have to catch the bus.'

Rose checks the time on her phone. 'It's still early. I'll catch the bus. What nerd-ing activities have you got on?'

It doesn't even bother Olive when Rose refers to her as a nerd. If anything, she likes the title. 'I'm tutoring some Year Nine girls in maths, have a meeting with Mrs Hammond about a practise essay I've asked her to read, and I told Ms Lyons I'd help set up the library for the leadership talk.'

'All before classes start?'

'All before classes start,' Olive confirms as she leans across her sister to put toothpaste on her toothbrush. Rose holds out her toothbrush for Olive to put paste on too.

'You know you don't have to do it all?'

Olive just stares at her sister, her lips twisted, wishing she had one ounce of the easy-going spirit Rose has. Olive wishes she didn't feel the need to put up her hand and offer help every time it was asked for. She wishes she could turn a blind eye to it all. She wishes the words 'I can do it' didn't fall out of her mouth so easily. She wishes she could choose herself over everyone else, but she never, ever does.

'I'm just saying, you're going to burn yourself out.' Rose holds up her phone and snaps a photo of the two of them in the mirror, toothbrushes wedged into their mouths with paste foaming at the edges. 'Sisters who brush together…' she types, uploading it online.

Olive wants to say, 'I know'. She wants to admit how terrified she is of running herself into the ground and how scared she is that she's going to crash so hard that it'll be impossible to recover. But instead she says, 'I'm fine.'

'Want to go for a swim?'

Olive considers, which in itself is unlike her, given the mountain of homework in front of her. It's only spring, but it's a stifling hot day and the ocean would be amazing. She ignores the longing to have the waves wash over her, and shakes her head. 'I washed my hair this morning.' She also straightened it because she had a speech assessment earlier in the day.

'Yeah? So wash it again.'

Olive's eyes fall on her homework schedule. She has hours of revision to do tonight after dinner. She really doesn't have time to wash her hair again.

'*Olive*, come on. It's about a billion degrees,' Rose moans. 'Just come for a swim with me!'

Fifteen minutes later, the two sisters are at the beach. They float in the water, which feels like silk against their skin, and peer up at the big clouds in the distance. The waves are calm as the girls somersault around and around, washing away the day.

'Remember how we used to do this when we were kids?' Rose says. 'We were going to be mermaids when we grew up,' she laughs.

Olive smiles. It really wasn't that long ago. They'd been best friends. They did everything together and even though they had always been different in their ways, it hadn't bothered them.

As they head back into the shore, Rose suggests they make a sandcastle. Olive's usual reaction would be to roll her eyes, but instead, she finds herself down on the sand, digging with her bare hands. The two sisters shape the sand into an impressive castle, complete with a moat for the incoming tide to fill. They collect seashells, sticks and seaweed to decorate it.

'I wish I had my phone to take a photo,' Olive says.

But Rose shrugs the suggestion away. 'We'll just take a snapshot in our heads, so we can remember it forever.' The words fall out of Rose's mouth so naturally. Olive's sure if she tried to say anything like that she'd just sound like an idiot.

But then they both just stand there, taking in their castle and its beautiful coastal backdrop. Rose leans in, putting her head on Olive's shoulder and wrapping an arm around her waist. Olive relaxes into Rose. She feels herself smiling.

'We better get home,' Olive says eventually, big, dark clouds now rolling in overhead.

They begin up the beach to collect their towels as the rain starts. They haven't even reached the dunes when it comes pouring down. They start running, the wild weather hitting hard. The sisters can't help but laugh as the wind tries to knock them over and the rain pelts down on their skin. They run the whole way home, leaving a trail of laughter behind them.

When they get home, they collapse onto the kitchen floor, dripping with water, but their faces aching with grins.

'I haven't laughed that hard in ages,' Rose declares, resting her head against the cupboards.

Olive considers, 'I don't think I've ever laughed that much.'

Olive's sitting at the kitchen bench—one of her favourite places to study—while her mum gets dinner ready. Rose drifts into the kitchen, her bare footsteps light against the floor, bringing with her the sweet scent of vanilla.

'Where are you off to, darling?' Their mother's voice fills the air.

Olive looks up from her books and sees Rose dressed in a

floaty dress, her long hair straightened, her lashes thick with mascara.

'Tom Henderson's Eighteenth.'

Olive looks back down at her books, trying not to think about it. It's been the hot topic of conversation at school all week.

'Oh, Olive, do you remember when Tom gave you a Valentine's Day card when you were in primary school?' their mum says. 'What a sweetheart.'

'Yes, Mum, I remember.' Olive keeps her voice level.

'He's always had a bit of a thing for you.'

Olive can feel her cheeks warming. She knows he's got a soft spot for her. He asked her during the week if she was coming to his party. She'd seen the hope in his eyes.

'Surely you're coming?' Rose smiles a little suggestively.

But he's too popular for her and she'd be a total disappointment if they started going out. 'I'm kind of studying for some really huge exams coming up. The HSC? You might have heard of it?'

Rose groans. 'Live a little.'

'You do plenty of that for the both of us.'

Rose doesn't seem to realise the comment is a criticism, or if she does, she doesn't let it bother her. 'It's going to be the biggest party of the year.'

Olive exhales loudly. 'Because I haven't heard that phrase before.'

'Your entire school year will be there. Give yourself the

night off study and have fun for once in your life.' Rose rolls her eyes.

'Because standing around in some paddock in the dark drinking cheap wine is *so much fun.*' Olive doesn't usually go for sarcasm, but she can't help herself.

Rose goes to say something else, but their mum sighs, 'Girls, that's enough.'

Olive wakes up with a jolt. She eyes the clock: it's right on curfew. She listens for a few moments, wondering if she heard Rose get home. She expects the usual sounds of her banging about in the kitchen, cooking two-minute noodles or cheese on toast.

But there's silence.

Olive pushes out of bed and opens her door. Rose's door on the opposite side of the hall is wide open, as she left it. Olive knows there's no point trying to get back to sleep when Rose is going to wake her any minute.

She grabs her phone from her bedside table and starts scrolling through the photos that have been posted that night from the party.

Rose hasn't posted anything, but she's in lots of other people's photos. Her arms draped around her friends, big smile, striking silly poses, laughing, carefree, thoughts of study so far from her mind. Olive wishes she knew what that felt like.

Twenty minutes pass and Rose still isn't home. It's not the first time she's missed curfew. Olive notices a new live stream in her Instagram feed. She clicks on it to watch a close-up of a guy from Rose's year grinning at the camera. He's pretending to be a news reporter, commentating on who hooked up with who at Tom's party. Olive doesn't want to waste brain cells filling her head with gossip, and is about to flick past it when a voice off camera interrupts. 'Shit! The cops are up ahead.'

The guy in frame turns, dropping his 'reporter' character as he looks away from the camera. 'Is that an ambulance too?'

Olive's stomach immediately tenses. The camera now jerks as the car visibly slows down. Her heart begins to beat faster as she sees the flicker of red and blue from a police car. But then the live feed goes dark when the phone is dropped into its owner's lap. Olive's stomach churns as she listens to the muffled voices.

'Whose car is it?'

'Dunno. It's so mangled.'

There's movement on screen as the owner picks up the phone again, but then the feed just stops, automatically scrolling to the next Insta story. Olive flicks back, desperately watching the footage again. She tries to see if it's Rose's car. *Their* car. But the footage is too dark.

Her hand begins to shake as she exits Instagram and clicks into her contacts to call Rose.

Pick up, pick up, pick up.

But each long ring is left unanswered.

Lead sinks in Olive's stomach as her panicked breathing flutters in the back of her throat. Her fingers fly over her phone.

'*Where are you? Saw there was an accident on Ocean Drive. Ring me!*'
Then adds, after a moment, '*Please!*'

Olive stares at her phone, waiting, willing Rose to call her, message her, anything. She clicks back to her Instagram feed to see if Rose has posted anything.

Nothing…

Until there is a knock on the door.

Hope fills Olive's mind as she imagines herself running to the front door, finding out that Rose got a lift home with someone else because she lost her keys.

But Olive just lies there, too scared to move. What if it isn't Rose at the door?

She hears her mum move down the hall.

Olive bites down on her lip, terrified to let her breath escape.

The murmur of strange voices cements the fear that's been growing in the pit of her stomach.

An ear-piercing sob.

The rush of her dad's footsteps.

More words exchanged.

Olive hurries now and makes it down the hall to see her mum collapse onto the floor, wailing in unnerving pain. Through the front window, Olive sees the haze of red and blue lights from the police car.

All the Days After

There's a blur of people at Rose's funeral. Phrases like 'lost too soon' and 'she's one of the angels now' keep floating through the air. Olive has to stop herself from screaming at the words. Don't these people realise she doesn't want Rose to be with the angels? She wants her to be across the hall cutting out magazines and being happy with her big dreams.

Olive stands next to her mum and dad, who thank people for coming, with tears in their eyes. Her parents nod as everyone tells them how wonderful Rose was, about the spark she brought to any occasion. That she was loving and fun and adored by all. Olive mindlessly thinks about what people would say about her. *I didn't really know Olive Atkins, but she got very good grades. Smart girl, dedicated to her studies…* Before all this, Olive probably would have felt that kind of reflection would be admirable, but now she just feels disappointed in herself.

People hug her to them, but she feels limp in their arms. She knows they're trying to offer her kindness, but she just wishes they'd go away.

She can feel people watching her, but she averts her eyes. Her mouth has no taste for words anymore. She quietly slips away from the crowd and hides herself behind some large potted plants at the end of the funeral home verandah. She tries to steady her breath as she pushes away images of the afternoon she shared with Rose at the beach only a week ago. Rose's words, *'We'll just take a snapshot in our heads, so we can remember it forever,'* play on repeat. The image is so clear that for a split second she can pretend Rose is still here. Olive hadn't felt as happy as she had that afternoon since she was a kid, and now she can't imagine ever being happy again. Going over every detail of that afternoon is like having one leg in scalding water, the other under a refreshing waterfall; she can't quite figure out whether it brings her more pain or more relief.

From her hiding spot, Olive watches the crowd. There are so many of them spilling out of the funeral home. She knows she shouldn't compare herself but wonders how many people would have been sad to see her die. If anything, they would have been sad for Rose, they would have come to Olive's funeral for *Rose's* sake. Poor Rose who had lost her sister.

She takes another deep breath as she sees Rose's mass of good friends. They're tear-stained and hugging, arms draped around one another. Some dropped into the house over the past few days, most bringing meals their parents made, all of them wanting to say how much they'll miss Rose. Her parents asked them questions, desperate to know as much as they could about Rose's last hours alive.

But no one knows why there was an accident. The investigation showed that Rose hadn't been drinking, wasn't using her phone in the car, wasn't speeding. But for some reason, her car rammed head-on into a tree on the side of the road.

Had a kangaroo jumped out in front of her?

Had another car been involved but fled the scene?

Had she been reaching for something on the passenger-side floor?

They didn't know the answer. Would never know the answer. And for Olive, this seemed unbearable. Every time she thought about it, there was a tightening across her chest.

Olive sees Tom Henderson and wonders what would have happened if she'd gone along to his Eighteenth. Olive would have driven, not Rose. Would they have made it home? She closes her eyes for just a second, trying to keep the guilt away.

He must sense that she's staring at him, because he looks directly up at her. They lock eyes. He looks handsome in a suit. Olive wonders if it's the same suit he planned on wearing to their Year Twelve Formal in a few weeks' time.

He starts towards her. She knows he wants to talk to her but, instead, she turns and quickly walks away, off the verandah and into the carpark. She wonders if he'll follow her.

But he doesn't.

Days pass. Weeks pass. Olive walks around in a haze. She keeps thinking, *This isn't real. I'm going to wake up from this.* She's numb to everything. She's cried, of course she's cried. She's never felt sadder, but still, she's waiting for it—for the grief to truly hit her. She can't imagine a life without Rose. She can hear her voice so clearly and sees her in every room of the house. But Olive fears there will be a time when she won't hear her voice, won't see her face, and knows her whole world is going to come crashing down.

Life without Rose.

Life without Rose.

It doesn't seem like a life worth living.

~

While the rest of her year finish their exams, Olive stays at home. While the rest of her year celebrates the end of school, Olive stays at home. She wonders if it would have been the same if Rose was still alive. Olive probably would have celebrated thirteen years of school by reading a book, rather than partying with everyone else. She imagines Rose rolling her eyes, telling her to let loose *for once*.

Olive's results come back. Thankfully, the school principal was able to organise 'misadventures' so that she would still receive her HSC, based on her averages over the course of the year. Her marks are good—great, actually, as everyone would have expected. But there's no satisfaction.

She defers uni. Her parents tell her she should still go, that it'd be good for her. But she says she can't, and her parents drop the subject.

The house is quiet, the walls dripping in sadness. Her parents go back to work, not sure what else to do.

And Olive is all alone. After always having a plan, she has no idea what to do with herself and all the years stretching out ahead of her.

Olive regularly looks back through Rose's Instagram photos. Most of them offer her comfort, maybe even a sense of contact. She spends hours clicking through them. It's just Rose's last post she tries not to look at—a selfie Rose took before going to Tom's party. She'd captioned it 'Party ready!' and is pouting at the camera, a cheeky glint in her eye. Olive's stomach always turns thinking back to that night in the kitchen before Rose left… Her long hair, her floaty dress, her eyes blinking out through a forest of mascara. Why didn't Olive just leave her books for one night and go with Rose? Why was she so scared of having fun? Of being a social disappointment? Of not being the best at school? The questions haunt her. She wishes she had a chance to redo that night. Maybe things would be different…

One day, Olive finds herself looking back through her own photos. At first she's filled with a dull disappointment at the photos that supposedly portray her life. But then, as she clicks onto each one, she sees that @_rose_atkins had liked every single one of her posts. In a world where Olive always felt somewhat alone, she realises she was never alone at all. She always had Rose. Her sister had always been there for her.

Olive's eyes sting with tears and her whole body aches, the tidal wave of grief pulling her under. She lets herself be taken, the pain dragging her further and further down. She wonders if she'll ever be free from it.

Rose's bedroom door was open on the night she died. But now the door is shut. Olive can't remember when it happened. Whether it was a couple of days after or a couple of weeks. Her mum goes in there most nights and lies on Rose's bed, often crying herself to sleep. Olive listens to her from her own room, wishing she could go and comfort her, but she doesn't want to intrude.

Olive hasn't wanted to go in there. She's been too scared

to go in there. But for some reason, today she finds herself opening the door.

Oh. A small sound escapes her mouth as she sees it's exactly the same as Rose left it. Clean, though. Her mum must have dusted and placed things back where they were. Jewellery spilled out onto her dresser, a half-read book on her bedside table, even some clothes crumpled on the floor near the wardrobe.

She sits at Rose's desk, not wanting to lie in the space that offers her mum comfort. Olive looks up at the pinboard that Rose had been working on. Olive hadn't paid much attention to it after that first day when she'd criticised Rose's dream of going to Paris.

A lump forms in her throat, wondering why she felt like she always had to point out the flaws in Rose's ideas. Why hadn't she been able to say something nice?

The pinboard is full of glitter and bright colours. 'Weird and Wacky Tour' is written in thick, loopy letters at the top. The board hosts a map of Australia, with little post-its pinned all over. Olive finds her fingers tracing over Rose's handwriting.

Coffs Harbour—Eat a banana at The Big Banana!
Mount Gambier—Dip my toes in the BLUE Lake!
Wave Rock—Pretend to surf the granite formation!
Talbot Bay—Jet boat ride through the Horizontal Water Falls!
Coober Pedy—Supposed to look like Tatooine from Star Wars!!!
Wycliffe Well—The UFO capital of Australia! (How cool?!)

The exclamation marks after every place bring a small smile to Olive's face, imagining her sister's excitement as she uncovered all the amazing places she wanted to go. All the dreams she had. All the places Rose had mentioned and so many more. Even the Dog on the Tuckerbox.

And just like that. Olive knows her dreams have changed.

Five Months Later

'Would you mind taking a photo for me?'

The woman nearby smiles, 'Of course,' and takes Olive's phone.

Olive steps back towards the statue and can't help but laugh as the woman snaps her photo.

'You look happy,' the woman comments, handing her phone back.

'It's a photo for my sister,' Olive says, her heart tugging as it always does. But as Olive visits each place on the Weird and Wacky Tour she can feel Rose there with her. Rose's tour has become *their* tour.

'It's much smaller than I thought it would be.' Olive gestures to the Dog on the Tuckerbox. She wonders if Rose realised how small it was.

The woman nods. 'Hope it's not a letdown?'

Olive shakes her head as she stares at the statue. 'No way. It's cool!' She finally gets what Rose had been going on about.

The woman walks off. Olive holds her phone up to take another photo, this time a grinning selfie with the Dog on the

Tuckerbox positioned over her shoulder. If she stares hard enough at the photo, she can see Rose in the picture too. She tilts her head back, letting the sun warm her face. She closes her eyes, fresh air filling her lungs, a soft calmness sweeping through her body.

#WorldHereICome.

About the Authors

Fleur Ferris (Foreword)

Fleur Ferris worked sixteen years in police and ambulance services in Victoria and South Australia before pursuing a career in writing crime fiction. Fleur is now the best-selling, award-winning and internationally published author of YA thrillers *Risk*, *Black*, *Wreck* and *Found*.

Fleur is pursuing studies in screenwriting and editing her debut novel for the middle grade audience, which will be released by Penguin Random House Australia in 2019.

Sofia Casanova

Sofia is a writer, editor and blogger based in Sydney. She works in publishing and can always be found with a cup of tea in her hand. Her writing has been featured on *Meanjin* and *Junkee*, and she frequently tweets @sofiaecasanova.

Cassi Dorian

Cassi is a Melbourne author who is currently studying Creative Writing at a Masters level. Her journey towards studying writing was an odd one, and in her undergraduate years she swapped out of a course for Aerospace Engineering to pursue her passion for the arts. She is a proud Slytherin, and in her spare time enjoys watching reruns of *The Simpsons*, which she often quotes to the annoyance of everyone around her.

Find out more on Cassi's Instagram @cassidorianbooks

Michael Earp

The book industry has claimed Michael's career. Between being a children's and YA specialist bookseller and a sales and marketing representative for a children's publisher, he has passionately worked with children's and YA books for more than half his life. A teacher who never taught because he couldn't bring himself to leave the book industry, he's a bit of a fanboy of Queer YA.

His writing has appeared in *The Victorian Writer* and *Aurealis*. He also established the #AusQueerYA tumblr to coincide with the #LoveOzYA campaign. He is the editor of *Kindred: 12 Queer #LoveOzYA Stories*, due out in 2019.

michaelearp.net, @littleelfman

Jes Layton

Jes (23, she/he) is a geek with a hat. Born on Gulidjan land, now living on Wurundjeri. Jes writes about and draws queer-nerdy things. She is the Administration Officer for the Melbourne City of Literature office, a freelancer, and a YA writer/advocate. Her work has been published in *The Victorian Writer*, *Reading Victoria*, *Others: An RMIT Anthology*, and online (under several dozen pseudonyms). He has appeared at several lit festivals around Melbourne discussing fanfiction and online fan culture. Try as he might, Jes is unable to keep his houseplants alive for very long. Send your condolence GIFs to @AGeekwithaHat (Twitter/Insta).

Sophie L Macdonald

Sophie is an English author who uses her background in psychology to delve into the darker corners of her characters' minds. She has a love of all things twisty, beautiful, weird, and uneasy, and will probably be a suspect if anything criminally strange happens in her local village.

She writes short stories for both print and online publications, and her debut YA dark fantasy novel, *Theatre of Illusions*, will be published in 2019 by 1231 Publishing. You can find her short stories in the anthologies *Futurevision, Obliquity* and *The Evil Inside* by 1231 Publishing, as well as in *Seasons of Discontent* by Needle in the Hay.

sophielmacdonald.com, Twitter: @SophieLMac.

Tobias Madden (Editor)

Tobias is a writer, editor, and proud Hufflepuff. Originally from Ballarat, Tobias has spent the past 10 years working as a singer/dancer/actor, touring Australia and New Zealand with musicals such as *Mary Poppins*, *CATS*, and *Guys and Dolls*. In recent times, he rekindled his childhood passion for writing, and shifted his attention to the world of publishing. In 2017, he was given the opportunity to edit an indie short story anthology called *WOLVES*, and to typeset another, called *Seasons of Discontent*, both for Needle in the Hay. Feeling as though he should use his new skills for the powers of Good, Tobias set to work on the *Underdog* project. *Underdog* is Tobias's first commercial undertaking as an editor, and he hopes that what started out as a very humble idea will grow into something much bigger: a platform for unpublished #LoveOzYA writers to showcase their work and have their voices heard.

tobiasmadden.net

Insta: @tobias_madden

Stacey Malacari

Stacey is a Queer writer from Perth, Western Australia. She is the founder of *Get YA Words Out*, a platform supporting the reading, writing and publishing of Australian Queer YA fiction. Stacey loves dystopian fiction, vegetarian cooking, coffee, wine, being hilarious, spending time with her family, cool socks, going on adventures, and all things Queer-culture. She cares strongly about fighting social injustices, particularly in the Queer community, taking care of people, our planet and animal rights. *The Bees* was inspired by, and co-edited with, her partner, Paris. It is a reflection on the complexity of families, on appreciating what you have and choosing love over fear. More simply, in the words of Frida Kahlo, 'Viva la vida'.

Felicity Martin

Felicity was born with a teaspoon in one hand and a pen in the other. She has been known to wield both these items savagely and with great aplomb. Noting the lack of writing about and by LGBT+ authors, she started the blog *Are There Lesbians?*, which judges books, films and video games on just one quality: whether or not there are lesbians. Since then, Felicity has expanded her writing into the freelance sector but maintains an interest in Queer rights and pop-culture. She has managed to combine all of these interests with a burgeoning love of the horror genre in her website *Strange Queer Things*. Felicity has BA in English (Hons) and History, which she uses to argue about medieval literature on the internet.

Kaneana May

Kaneana studied Television Production at university and graduated with honours in screenwriting. She went on to work in television, including roles as a script assistant on *All Saints*, a storyliner on *Headland*, and a scriptwriter on *Home and Away*. She's now focusing her attention on writing both young adult and contemporary women's fiction. Her debut women's fiction (or 'lifelit') novel, *The One*, is due for release in July 2019 (Harlequin). Kaneana lives on the Mid North Coast of NSW with her husband and three children. For more about Kaneana, check out kaneanamay.com or join her over on Facebook and Instagram.

KM Stamer-Squair

KM Stamer-Squair is a Literary Studies graduate from Monash University. In 2017, she spent her honours year looking at the relation between anthropocentricism and environmental degradation. She dreams of nurturing a self-sustaining garden, quotes *Hamlet* with too much enthusiasm, and lives surrounded by piles of books.

Sarah Taviani (Assistant Editor)

Sarah is an editor, writer and social media manager. She studied literature in her undergrad and post-grad, and is now suffering from an acute case of HECS debt. While she hasn't won any awards for her writing yet, she has come first at several *Harry Potter* trivia nights. *Mediocre Heroes* is her first published work of fiction.

Sarah also takes way too many photos of books; visit Commas and Ampersands on Instagram for more.

Vivian Wei

Vivian is currently studying architecture at the University of Technology, Sydney. She enjoys all things in shades of yellow and loves exploring the arts and design world. In her spare time, Vivian likes to take photos of friends and food—but mostly the latter. *The Chinese Menu for the Afterlife* is her first published short story.

Instagram: @omumeshi

Editor's Acknowledgements

Firstly, I'd like to thank the readers, writers, bloggers and Bookstagrammers of the #LoveOzYA community. You were the reason I dreamed up this crazy scheme in the first place. A book is nothing without someone to read it, so thank you for supporting local authors by picking up a copy of *Underdog*! Your encouragement throughout the whole process has been truly overwhelming and has taken my little idea and turned it into something really wonderful.

Thanks must go to Caitlin, Marilyn, Lauren, Elisabeth, Julia, and all at Black Inc/Nero; Alissa Dinallo, for our glorious cover; my big brother, Judd, for our awesome logo; Fleur Ferris, for her inspiring foreword; Centre for Youth Literature and The Little Bookroom for thier support; Karen Wyld, Michael Earp, Beau Kondos, and #LoveOzYA KWEEN Danielle Binks, for their wonderful advice; my *Underdog* team—Brylie Harris, Monique Deane and Sarah Taviani—who supported this idea from its inception through to its realisation; my fellow *Underdog* authors, who put their faith in me and trusted me with their precious words; my insightful, meticulous, and incomparable assistant editor, Sarah Taviani, without whom this anthology would never have made it to print; my incredible parents (and proofreaders extraordinaire) Vicki and Peter; and finally, my husband, Daniel, for believing in me wholeheartedly, every second of every day. You inspire me beyond belief, and I would never have achieved this without you by my side!

Tobias xoxo

Underdog.

underdogshortstories.com

@underdogshortstories

/underdogshortstories

We welcome school talk and workshop enquiries!

underdogshortstories@outlook.com

www.ingramcontent.com/pod-product-compliance
Lightning Source LLC
Chambersburg PA
CBHW020917060726
47591CB00004B/1285